Mary Joyce

John Clare's Muse

GW00708612

Mary Joyce

John Clare's Muse

A novel

Russell C Carter

Blenheim Press Limited
Codicote

© Russell C Carter 2009

Russell C Carter has asserted his right to be identified
as the Author of this work.

Published in 2009 by
Blenheim Press Ltd
Codicote Innovation Centre
St Albans Road
Codicote
Herts SG4 8WH

ISBN 978-1-906302-12-2

Typeset by TW Typesetting, Plymouth, Devon

Printed and bound by CPI Antony Rowe, Eastbourne

The author dedicates this book to Rosemary, Bill and Ben,
in gratitude for friendship and encouragement,
and in memory of my Major;
without whom there would have been no acquaintance.

ACKNOWLEDGEMENTS

The author wishes to acknowledge the information regarding Mary Joyce's demise obtained from the late Keith Traynar, from the many people who have written biographies of John Clare, and from John Clare himself for his own autobiographical writings.

Also I must thank Mrs G. Wells for reading and typing my handwritten manuscript, and to Mrs R. Kynnersley, for also reading and commenting on my book. I am deeply grateful to all concerned.

ONE

The confinement took place at Christmas 1796. Mrs Joyce lay in her cut down four-poster bed that had once graced a much loftier room, but fate had decreed it pass to the family, and despite living in a substantial stone built house, the alteration had to take place. The fire cast a warm red glow on the highly polished oak furniture and a few flakes of snow fluttered by the leaded light window.

The tiny infant, a girl, lay securely wrapped up, by her mother's side. They had decided to name her Mary. It was a well used family name passed down from generation to generation. Mrs Joyce was a farmer's wife. Her husband, James, owned the Joyce's Farm, in the quaint village of Glinton, very near the border of Northamptonshire and Lincolnshire's flat fen lands, with rich soil and a view that you could see for miles, especially if you climbed the tower of Glinton church and stepped out at the base of its needle spire. James Joyce had done such a thing many times, for he was a church warden. His name, cmblazoned in big deeply carved letters, was on one of the roof beams, in clear view of those sitting in the pews. The church and his religion came second place to his passion for his farm. He was bible thumper of the first order and he insisted his family and workers attend services on a regular basis.

He had only just closed the chamber door on his wife and baby daughter after telling her the date of the baptism had already been arranged. It was to be on the 10th of January 1797 and nothing would intervene for the ceremony not to take place. Mrs Joyce knew better than argue with her husband; he always got his own way in all matters. Besides she was tired after this birth, she hoped it would be the last.

Her mother had always said the wife should have the first baby, and the husband the second, and that would be that! James had provided a good home and security, not to mention fortune for her and the children. He was kind in his way with them, fair to his workers and would not see any of them want in times of hardship. He was now in the parlour telling the children to play as quiet as mice, since their mother needed to sleep and rest so she could get up as soon as possible. He took down the old bible from its accustomed shelf of the bookcase, laid it on his desk, took the pen, dipped it in the inkwell and inscribed his new offspring's name and date following the long list of other names and dates. 'All for Posterity' he thought. After the ink was dry he read a chapter, then turned his attention to the newspaper. He was glad he was an Englishman, as he never tired of telling his neighbours – That Frenchie lot! Barbarians the lot of them with their bloody revolution, murdering thousands, including the King and Queen, and then turning on that monster Robespierre, and now a Corsican soldier was taking the news with his exploits, what next, would the man proclaim himself King? It did not bear thinking about.

There had been a good fall of snow in the night. The villagers awoke to a magical winter wonderland. The baptism was set for the afternoon and there was to be food and drink provided for all comers, afterwards. All Farmer Joyce's workforce were invited and as a show of appreciation they one and all spent several hours clearing a path through the snow, from the front door of the house, down the streets, across the churchyard to the church door, so no one would slip and fall. Heavy shawls were placed near the fires to take the heat, and only moments before they left, the tiny infant was carefully wrapped up against the cold, as was her mother. It was a great success, all parties safe and sound on the cleared pathway, the vicar bestowing the single name 'Mary', the child not making a murmur, the procession retiring to an ample and orderly feast. The Joyce family were happy and content. 'Couldn't have gone better' said James to his wife in bed that night and they warmly embraced.

The new baby survived (it was a time when infant mortality was quite high). She prospered and grew, her eyes remained blue and her hair, when it grew in profusion, was fair. Blessed also with a fine doll-like complexion and in the course of time a contented and placid nature. Mary proved to be the fourth and final child of Ann and James Joyce. There were two boys, William and James and another girl, Ann. The Joyces all down the generations had no imagination for Christian names and used the same formula over and over again in rigid monotony. Mary was the darling as well as the baby of the family, they all doted on her and helped their mother bring her up, and their reward was a sweet and gentle-natured child, who in turn learnt quickly and in the years to come did whatever she could to help in the running of the family home.

Despite his prosperous farm and business acumen, Farmer Joyce fully believed in a solid education, in reading, writing and arithmetic. He had no time for such like things as the gentry indulged in, like making music or painting or drawing, and as long as a woman could clean a house, put a decent meal on the table and wash and sew, those attributes for the gentle sex were sufficient. Mary was helped in reading by all members of the family, in readiness for when she could attend school.

The elder siblings had all been educated by the village schoolmaster, a Mr Seaton, and the 'school' was held in the vestry of Glinton church, a compact but lofty whitewashed room with a few time-worn benches and tables and a large piece of dirty discoloured matting which disguised a large black tombstone to the memory of a gentleman by the name of Wing, above whose long decayed bones the children learnt their lessons. Mr Seaton was a well-respected member of the village community and had been the schoolmaster for several decades, and the majority of the villagers had been taught in this small vestry by him.

Mr John Seaton was at this moment sitting in his old elbow chair noting every child who entered the vestry, and here was a new one! A small pale fair-haired little girl with her sister Ann, already a tried and tested pupil. Mr Seaton arranged his pupils into age and ability groups and soon found out the levels of intelligence and knowledge possessed by all parties. Mary seemed more intelligent and co-operative than her older sister. She possessed a strong depth of observation not always associated with a child of her tender years. Learning quickly and well she was soon at the top of her age group. James and Ann Joyce were greatly pleased.

TWO

Time passed, the seasons came and went, and one day on entering the schoolroom, she stumbled and let fall a book she had been lent by the master, when a small brown hand reached out and picked up the volume for her. She looked up into the face of a boy she had never seen before in her life. His hair was a pale copper colour, his body small and thin, his face white, with fine delicate features and small deep-set blue eyes. The boy handed her the book. Mary stared at him, then, quickly remembering her manners, whispered, 'Thank You.'

She took her accustomed place on the form, the boy on the form behind her, a few feet away, and lessons commenced. Suddenly, as an afterthought, Mr Seaton said, 'Children, we have a new pupil today, you will not have seen him before as he does not reside in Glinton. This is John Clare. Please to assist and make him welcome.' Smiles and nods went round the little room. In the course of lessons and examining his new pupil, Mr Seaton quickly realised the boy was considerably above the intelligence of the present class, but he gave no indication of his opinions. When the time came for a break in the proceedings, the children trooped out into the churchyard, which also served as their playground. They were all eager to speak to the new boy and find out where he came from, since he was a total stranger to one and all. Mary kept her ears open as he patiently answered their probing. He had walked two whole miles along a bridle path across the common grazing meadows from the little village called Helpstone.

No, his father was not a farmer, he was a labourer, who could sing about a hundred ballads all learnt by heart, and he was a renowned wrestler in the community. He had a pet cat and a sparrow, and the two lived together and were friends! There was much disbelief at this statement. Why, it was quite outrageous! But the boy insisted it was the truth. Mary watched his face, it had an open honest expression and she knew he was not lying.

4

The days passed. It was not possible for him to attend all the lessons, due to seasonal jobs as required to earn money to help his parents, to put food on the table and pay the rent of the tenement, the part of the old cottage which he lived in. Despite his irregular schooling, John Clare forgot nothing and brought in completed work for Mr Seaton, who gave out little rewards for the best work and lent books from his personal library. Mary managed to steal a moment or two and have short conversations. She found out he had a younger sister, Sophy, but no brothers. He had been a twin, but the baby girl died about two weeks after the birth, and another baby girl had died also in infancy. She was lucky having a sister and two strong brothers, who she knew would grow up to be farmers like their father, and why, she herself might become a farmer's wife, or even marry a man of much higher station in life than the Joyce family enjoyed. But the more she got to know John Clare, the more she felt he was a true kindred spirit. Mary loved the storybooks of the time, and her parents encouraged her reading. Then one day something wonderful happened. John Clare came to school carrying a volume of poetry: it was *The Seasons* by James Thomson.

Mr Seaton knew of this most famous work of the previous century, and desired John to read aloud to the class a portion of the work. He turned a little red, but stood in front of the forms with the volume open in his hands, and recited. Mary was enthralled. The description of the countryside put into such language was a revelation for her, but then there was also the fascination of hearing her new classmate and friend, John Clare, with his clear expressive voice bringing the work to life. The tears stood in her beautiful blue eyes as she listened and hastily brushed then away, lest any thought her a fool. Her actions and emotions were not lost on the reader, who somehow took in all he saw and analysed in a single glance. At the end, the master praised him warmly, and a murmur of approval and quite unheard of appreciation circled the small audience.

On the first opportunity, Mary said to John, 'How did you know about that book?'

'Well,' he replied, 'a boy I know showed me a copy he had, and I read the first lines, and I had to have my own copy, so I teased the money out of my father, and walked to Stamford and bought it.' Mary was impressed with the fact that he walked so very far. She had *only* been once to Stamford and twice to Peterborough, on shopping expeditions with her family in the pony trap. Stamford she much preferred to Peterborough, although the latter had a massive cathedral, but she did not like it, too black looking and vast for her taste. It was only an old market town, whereas Stamford had more and much finer shops. She decided that when the time came for another excursion to Stamford, she would ask her parents if they would allow her to look in a bookshop and see and choose a book for herself. She also craved Thomson's *Seasons*.

A few days later, Mary made some attempt at conversation with John. She asked him about Helpstone, what it was like, what he did with his time when not working. He told her he preferred his solitary rambles in the fields and woods, and there was a brook that may once have been a small river, with a heavy wooden plank across serving as a bridge, where he loved to stand or sit and look and listen to all the sounds of nature. He was perfectly happy doing this, with the gentle bubbling of the stream beneath him. Later Mary asked her parents about Helpstone.

'Helpstone,' said her father, 'is a small poor place, not as large or as fine as Glinton. They do have a good church but you cannot see it at a great distance as you can ours. Why do you ask, child?'

'There is a boy comes to school from there.'

'What is his name Mary?' said her mother.

'John Clare,' she answered.

'Clare? Are they farmers?' asked Mr Joyce.

'No, Mr Clare is a labourer, and they live in a little cottage.'

'Well,' said Mrs Joyce, 'they must have high hopes for their son.'

'Mr Seaton is most pleased with his work,' said Mary.

'That he is too,' this from Mary's sister Ann, 'and I overheard him telling Tim Smith that he is friends with a family that owns a telescope and that they allow him to use it and look at the moon and stars.'

'Bless my soul!' said Mr Joyce. 'Then he mixes with real gentry.'

'And they must think highly of him too,' said his wife.

Mary was secretly pleased with how this conversation had gone. It showed this poor boy, who came from such a humble home (hers was splendid by comparison), in the best possible light. 'And he wins all the prizes from Mr Seaton,' she said.

'Indeed?' asked Mrs Joyce.

'I do not think James or William ever won any awards for their time with Mr Seaton,' mused Mr Joyce.

'No, but Ann got one,' said his wife.

'Ah yes, so she did,' said he, 'I had quite forgotten – so much else to think about.' And the conversation turned to farming matters.

Mary lay in her bed, in the room she shared with her sister Ann, and thought about Helpstone. It was two miles to walk there, then two to walk back, that made four, but she wanted to see the cottage tenanted by the Clares. Then there was his sister Sophy, who was about the same age as herself, and what was this girl like? Maybe like John? She did not know. Also she desired to walk down the lane and see the woods, the birds' nests, the rabbits, the brook with the plank for a bridge, but then that meant walking a lot further, and the further you went, the same distance had to be traversed on the way back. She felt it was really a bit too far at the moment, and in any case her parents would never allow her to wander off so far on her own. She would have to have James or William to see as no harm came to her. It would be so nice to be grown up and please herself. She felt that it would happen one day and she would be her own mistress. Tiredness and sleep overcame her, and she dreamed of a path through a pretty meadow, full of daisies and buttercups.

THREE

A mature walnut tree grew in the garden of a near neighbour of the Joyces. The son of the house also attended Seaton's vestry school. He had pulled a quantity of unripe walnuts from the tree, and with his pockets stuffed. went to school. In the churchyard away from old Seaton's prying eyes, the boy handed out the walnuts to his friends as gifts. John Clare was given one. Someone had the idea of pelting the hideous gargoyles that adorned the church roof. The last gargoyle at the end was a particular favourite of all the children. The stonemason who had carved and fitted the rest had not been paid the amount he had been promised, so in a spiteful rage he had carved not a grinning face like his others but the naked rear of a woman with her hands clasping either cheek, so that when it rained it looked just like a female urinating.

Children loved that opportunity to view the spectacle when it rained! None of the boys could throw so high as to hit any of the gargoyles, so they always aimed for a portion of wall with the least amount of glass. There had been a recent burial in the churchyard, and following heavy rainfall during the night the ground was muddy, so that John Clare slipped as he threw the green walnut and lost his balance. The missile, missing its mark, struck Mary a direct hit in the right eye. She let out a great scream, and Ann ran to see what the matter was.

John Clare picked himself up and stood for a moment transfixed in horror. Mary was in pain and crying bitterly. 'It was an accident,' he shouted. Then in fit of bravado, to show the other boys that he cared nothing for his rash act, he laughed. That was like a red rag to a bull to Ann who, letting go of Mary, ran and slapped his face as hard as she possible could. The others just stood openmouthed.

'Come, Mary, we are going home and mother can bathe your poor eye.'

Back into the vestry trooped the class. Mr Seaton looked up from the lesson he had just prepared. He saw two empty places that had been occupied a little while before. 'Where are Ann and Mary Joyce?'

demanded he of the class. A friend of Mary, one Jane Wells, spoke up. 'If you please Sir, Mary is hurt and crying, so Ann took her home.'

'How is she hurt?' he asked.

'That new boy, John Clare, threw something and it hit her in the eye,' said Jane.

'And what did you throw, John Clare?' demanded the Master.

'We was throwing walnuts to see how far we could throw, but I slipped, and it hit Mary in the eye. I did not mean to do it.'

'Do you realise you could have knocked her eye out?' bellowed Seaton. 'This is an utter disgrace, you are in the house of God, you disport yourselves on sacred ground, you have no respect for the dead, none of you must ever act thus again. As for you, John Clare, I command that you go after class to call on Mr and Mrs Joyce and offer your abject apology for what you have done to their daughter, and if Mr Joyce chooses to take his horse whip to you, then that will be your just reward. I can only hope, on my part, that no lasting damage has been done to Mary, for as it says in the bible "An eye for an eye".'

The boy turned white, then red; he felt as sick as he ever felt in his short life. All eyes were on him after school as slowly walked out of the churchyard and turned in the direction of the Joyce's Farm. He did not dare approach the front door, but made his way round to the back, and knocked with the large brass ring knocker. Footsteps approached along the flagstone floor, and a young woman, very plain, opened the door. She wore a large mobcap and a dull brown dress. Two large eyes glared from the sallow face. 'Yes?' she demanded.

'Excuse me, I have called to ask how Mary be,' said John in an almost inaudible voice.

'Are you the wretch that hurt her?'

'Yes.'

'Come in here.' She grabbed him and pulled him into a large kitchen. 'Stay there,' she said. John stood. 'Mistress, Mistress!' she called at an open door that led to the hall and staircase. Obviously Mrs Joyce was upstairs with Mary.

'What is it Lizzie?' called down Mrs Joyce.

'If you please Ma'am, it's that brat that hurt Miss Mary.'

There was an exclamation of disgust. Down the stairs came Mrs Joyce, her daughter Ann following to see what action her mother would take against the culprit.

'Oh, so you are the so-called "clever boy" John Clare that has nearly

9

blinded my little Mary!' she cried. John wished the flagstones would open and swallow him up.

'It was an accident. I slipped on the mud and wet grass. I would not hurt Mary for the world. I am truly sorry, Mrs Joyce.'

'You stood and laughed at what you did.' This from young Ann. 'Not much sorry there.'

'If my daughter loses her sight because of you, it will mean prison for you, and make no mistake on that score, and we will soon know the worst for the doctor has been sent for, and your parents will have to pay his bill.' The tears streamed down the boy's pale face, his body was convulsed with sobs – to be parted from his parents! The horror of it, and his parents were so poor, they had to keep themselves, himself, Sophy, and his grandmother Alice. It was impossible.

'Oh, please, please, do not make my parents pay,' he begged. 'I will work for you and do anything to pay the doctor, I just want Mary better, so she will still be my friend.'

'Friend!' snorted Mrs Joyce. 'Some hope of that after what you did today Master Clare.'

And so the boy trudged slowly home, where they could plainly see that a great trouble had fallen on their son, and he was obliged to be honest and tell the tale. At length, Mrs Clare spoke. 'Boy, we can only pray the child's sight is not afflicted, and I only hope they let you work off your debt, or it's the poorhouse for us.'

Shock and fear went through all the members of the family as they awaited the doctor's verdict. Medical knowledge was still very poor in those days, and the doctor simply prescribed bathing the eye, complete rest and a darkened room, no bright sunlight, peace and quiet in general. At the end of a week the eye appeared normal but Mary could not bear to touch it for some considerable time. What the long-term effects would be would not surface for a great many years. The sum of the doctor's fee was never disclosed to John Clare.

Mr Joyce set him to work, to do jobs in his capability. He was treated with extreme coldness and at times great scorn, but that was all better than prison and the workhouse. Young Ann Joyce kept a close eye on Mary, she did not want here sister to speak or ever associate with John again. One day he would leave Glinton vestry school, and then there would never again be any cause for him to visit Glinton, she hoped. Eventually Farmer Joyce released the boy from his servitude, and it was providential he did, because there was work and wages awaiting him at Helpstone.

FOUR

Many months went by, John Clare helping his father in the old barn just across the lane from their cottage, or tending horses on the heath, or scaring crows, which all helped to pay the rent and put food on the table. In the evening he would pass on his learning to his sister Sophy, and in so doing saved the expense and journeys to and from Glinton.

When he did return to the school, he found Mr Seaton had retired due to ill health and age, and a new master, a Mr Merrishaw, had taken his place. Some students had left to earn their keep, a few young new ones had arrived. And then he saw Mary. He stared, and no wonder, she had literally blossomed from a very pretty child to a young beauty. She looked up from her book, and she almost smiled, but turned red and dropped her gaze to the book. She could not look or speak. It was impossible. Ann was still at school, and would scold her if she dared make any form of contact, tell the rest of the family, then that would mean the end of her school days, until the offending article, one John Clare, left for good and all.

The lessons commenced. In examining John's work and knowledge, Mr Merrishaw was pleasantly surprised. As time passed he set the boy harder and harder lessons and tasks, but John always excelled expectations, and was constantly rewarded. (Mr Merrishaw kept on the tradition begun by old Mr Seaton.) All this time, Mary Joyce sat only a few feet away, but never made any attempt to speak, many times she could see him gazing at her from the corner of her eye, but she must never lower herself to him. She might have lost the sight of one eye because of him, and no amount of money could have restored it, and with her obvious beauty marred, who in the world would want a one-eyed wife? She would have remained a spinster and been dependent on her brothers for support, and she wanted her position and independence above all things.

The day came when Mr Merrishaw said in front of the whole class, 'You can go home John Clare, for I can teach you nothing more.'

11

There was a general gasp, and the boy stood up and went forward.

'Thank you Sir, for all your help and kindness, I shall not forget it.' They shook hands, and as he took up his personal books and went to the door, he could not help but look at Mary, who had such a look of shock and surprise on her sweet face. Her sister Ann gave a 'Good riddance' glare, and then he was gone, gone for good, gone back to the miserable tenement, in the lowly cottage, in that poor village called Helpstone.

Ann Joyce gleefully told her mother the day's tidings. 'Thank God for small mercies!' said Mrs Joyce. 'Your father will be thankful when I tell him. Still, the boy did work and pay off the bill, and a lot more besides. Teach the little devil a good lesson, that did, I doubt if he will ever come to anything in life.' Ann laughed; it was her sentiments entirely. Now Mary could, in time, forget him, finish her education, and eventually find a nice young well-to-do gentleman who could provide a good home and all she was used to, and more besides, for a husband. Lying in her bed in the darkened bedroom, Mary went through a whole range of emotions. Part of her was glad he was gone for ever, but the stronger emotion was that she now missed his company. None of the other boys were an equal to him, and the worst of it was she could never confide her feelings to any member of her family for fear of ridicule.

At this time a change was to come over all England. Parliament had passed a new bill, the Enclosure Act. It was designed to increase productivity in farming, and it did so. With increase of crops and wealth, the common grazing land for the poor was taken away or 'enclosed', hedges were planted, No Trespassing signs went up. Well-to-do farmers like James Joyce got richer, people like the Clares only suffered more and found it harder to make even the most basic living. The Clares were even forced to sell the apples off their tree to pay the rent.

Ann Joyce was restless. She felt that she had had enough of school and that her real role in life was to be at home with her mother, and learn from her and from the servant Elizabeth Bird, the whole business of running a successful home, cooking, cleaning, washing, and keeping accounts as to the expenditure of same. She put this train of thought to her mother. Mrs Joyce agreed wholeheartedly, Mr Joyce said so be it, so Ann left the vestry school. Six months or so later, Mary did so too. At least, so Mrs Joyce thought privately, if that peculiar Clare boy came sniffing around, both girls would not be in so public a place. They were far more use at home, helping and learning to be good housewives, for that would no doubt be their place in life, to marry well and bring up children, just as she herself had done, and all females of her own family before her, down the centuries.

Mary Joyce had a good head for figures so she did a great deal to help her father with his book-keeping, labour wages, grain and feed costs. Both her brothers had for some considerable time been deeply involved with the running of the farm. James, as elder, would in time-honoured tradition take over the Joyce's Farm and become Farmer James the second. William wanted his own farm too, but that had to wait until there were sufficient profits to purchase one, and also both boys needed to find suitable wives who would bring in handsome dowries to help their husbands along this steep path.

At the village of Maxey, a few miles north of Glinton, lived the Clarks, also farmers, on friendly terms with the Joyces. The daughter of the house was called Ruth, and the son was Joe. Mr and Mrs Joyce both secretly hoped that James or William would marry Ruth, and that Joe would marry Ann.

On a day when he could afford to spend the time, Farmer Joyce rode over to see Mr Clark, who was by now a widower, pass the time of day and see how the land lay regarding his offspring.

FIVE

Mr Ben Clark was tending his late wife's flower garden when he heard the sound of horses' hooves. Looking up, he was overjoyed when he realised he was to have company and hear the latest gossip. The two men were sitting in the comfortable parlour, both with a pint of ale in front of them, discussing their respective farms, when the door opened quickly and Joe Clark came in quite breathless. He dropped into a chair.

'What be the matter, boy?' asked his father.

'I was told the news that Bonaparte has landed in England, and that he has marched on Northampton!' gasped the youth.

'My God!' exclaimed Mr Joyce.

Mr Clark was silent; things did not seem real or important to him since his Sarah had passed away.

'A fellow I know has passed by Peterborough and says the Prince Regent wants to recruit able bodied males age 18–45 years, volunteers,' continued Joe. 'The bounty is two guineas, or if drawn go for nothing! But how can I leave Ruth and father to run the farm?'

'Thou shalt not go,' said his father. 'Let that fat fop go, and do his own damned fighting, you be needed here, there's plenty can be dispensed with for cannon fodder!'

'My sentiments entirely,' said Mr Joyce. 'And if it comes to it, I will give an amount of cash to keep my boys with me, my farm is their inheritance, and should ill befall me, there are Ann and the girls to consider. Besides, who would do our jobs if we are not able? We provide food in various forms for the entire population, and if I came face to face with the Regent or his father, I would say exactly the same thing, and hang the consequences.'

'Bravo!' shouted Joe Clark. 'Thou should be in Parliament Mr Joyce!'

'Thank you Joe, that is most appreciated,' said James, and before anything else could be said the door opened again, and in walked Ruth. She was now a tall, reserved, pale-faced girl with blue eyes and naturally blonde hair. She had been working in the dairy and had heard the horses' hooves stop at the gate.

'Ruth. here is our good friend, Mr Joyce, come over from Glinton to see how we all be,' said Mr Clark.

'Good Day Sir,' said Ruth politely.

'Well Ruth, you have grown tall since I saw you last, and not married yet?'

Ruth blushed. 'Nay,' said her father, 'tis too soon for that, and besides I wants to see Joe wedded first, for he is eldest, and I wants a good girl like my poor Sarah was to run this place.'

'Aye, true,' said James. 'When you can all spare the time, please to all come to the Joyce's Farm and pay myself and my wife a visit, it will be a most welcome diversion.'

And so it was left. The rumours of the French invasion struck terror to all concerned, and a local militia was formed from all the villages in that area of Northamptonshire. Both the families of Joyce and Clark defended their young males due to their respective work, and were left in peace.

Mrs Ann Joyce decided to go to the market town of Peterborough to make certain purchases of a few new items for the family home, should her hopes be realised respecting a visit from the Clarks, and the possibility of a union betwixt these two families. William drove his mother in the pony trap, which they left in the care of the ostler at The Angel, while Mrs Joyce visited various emporiums. On leaving the town's main linen draper, they were forced to stand on the top step due to a great crowd of motley men marching past. All ages and in all states of attire, as they never beheld before or since, accompanied by uniformed officers on horseback, passed down narrow Bridge Street towards the ancient wooden bridge that spanned the River Nene, on their way to the town of Oundle for the formal training and billeting. Some faces were familiar, as they came from Glinton, and seeing the Joyces there were a few salutations.

Then William gasped, 'Mother, I have just seen that boy Ann and Mary went to school with. You remember, he hit Mary in the eye, and it hurt her so badly.'

'What, where?' said Mrs Joyce. William pointed, she looked. 'Yes Son, that is surely John Clare. Good for nothing, maybe the army will knock him into shape, for I did hear that he has no trade, cannot settle what he wants to do in life, and works at labouring like his father.'

'And if there is war,' said William, 'maybe it will be the end of him.'

'If it is, it is,' said his mother. 'That is God's will, and none can oppose it.'

William felt physically sick. All those men could be mown down, hard working, honest men, probably with wives and children, because some power-mad Corsican wanted to literally rule the world and rule England, usurping King George and his son, the Regent. And suppose it came about? Would the monster erect a guillotine in Hyde Park and despatch all and sundry to it as had been done in Paris?

The Joyces returned to Glinton, whereupon William set about unloading the purchases, and his mother went to find Ann and Mary, who were both dusting and polishing in the parlour.

'My dears, such a sight we saw in Peterborough . . .' she began. 'All these men marching with real soldiers, to learn the business of fighting Bonaparte, if he gets so far as this County, and William, he spotted a person you both know, who went to old Seaton's school, that boy Clare from Helpstone. Yes he's gone too. I can't say I feel sorry, although 'tis hard for his parents should there be war, and he be killed, but there it be. 'Tis fate, and none can gainsay it.'

Ann's mouth dropped open. Mary turned white. 'My God, mother,' said Ann, 'let's pray there is no war, we don't want James or William going off to get killed'. Mary sank into a chair, she felt faint to hear that name again after so long a period and under these circumstances it was quite overwhelming.

'You feel ill, Mary?' said her mother.

'I would like a glass of water, please.' She whispered. Ann ran and fetched it. Mary drank.

'Well, 'tis always a shock when things happen, or come close to it, when it's your own kin,' said Mrs Joyce. Mary's mind was in turmoil. It was unthinkable that England should be conquered by this French upstart or whatever he was supposed to be, and to lose either or both brothers in the process was something she could never come to terms with. But then there was the fascination and feelings that she always had entertained for John Clare. She could never, she was sure, discuss this last matter with any member of her family. She must overcome, smother, kill the feelings. She was destined to become the wife of someone of substance, not some poor peasant labourer who lived in poverty and squalor. 'Mary, go and lie down till you feels better, 'tis a warm day and I expects you have been polishing the furniture too vigorously,' said her mother. Ann walked behind her up the stairs, saw her settled on the bed, then left her. She had ideas, but were they the right ones? Ann hoped not.

SIX

The purchases from Peterborough were a great success. Mrs Joyce had chosen well. The main rooms now had more of comfort but with good taste and a homely feel besides. Mr Joyce was satisfied, it was money well spent. Should their plans regarding the Clarks come to nothing, there was plenty more of the farming community he could call upon in the matrimonial sense, and they could still enjoy their modestly refurbished home.

In due course a simple get together was planned, a day set aside, convenient to all parties, and the Clarks came over from Maxey to Glinton. The young people smiled and weighed each other up. First impressions always go a long way, and always will. Ruth took instantly to both Ann and Mary. Joe looked at Ann and felt that although she was the older of the sisters, she had more character and practicality for a future farmer's wife. Mary was distant, almost in another world. She lacked conversation, merely answering 'Yes' and 'No' or 'I am sorry I do not have an opinion on this subject' or 'I do not know'. James and William were not really taken with Ruth, she was like Mary, too quiet and reserved, but in wandering in the gardens all six young people enjoyed the day, there was no bad feeling or resentment of any kind, and Joe Clark felt he would like to see Ann Joyce again.

James and William conversed with Joe on the recent enclosure, and how it affected them, the running and difficulties of farming, and of course the militia and threat from France. They all had the same opinions and warmed to each other very well. James confided to William that night after the Clarks' departure that he would not mind Joe for a brother-in-law, and William agreed.

In the coming weeks and months Joe called on Mr and Mrs Joyce, and they got to know each other. He would walk and talk in the garden with Ann, always making sure they could be seen from the house windows, or if they wanted a stroll down the lanes and meadows, Mary would accompany then, and then discreetly walk on ahead without turning and looking back. Ann was always grateful to Mary for her help in this courtship. The upshot was a proposal from Joe and his acceptance from Ann. Both families were almost frantic with joy. There was simply just so much to do. Ann would, of course be married in Glinton church, and virtually the whole village would be in attendance.

In the bedchamber, Ann made a joke to Mary. 'It's a good thing that Joe did not propose to you, Mary!'

'Why?' said Mary, blushing.

'Well, fancy a Joseph marrying a Mary, and then they have a baby son – well, people would say – what's his name? – Jesus!!!'

Both girls collapsed on to the bed in shrieks of laughter, making so much noise that Mrs Joyce ran upstairs to find out the cause of the commotion.

'Oh' she gasped, 'don't let your father hear that, he would say it was blasphemy,' but she too laughed heartily enough.

The threat of invasion from France came, in the end, to nothing. Bonaparte never set foot on English soil. The Northamptonshire militia was disbanded, and the would-be and far from would-be soldiers quickly marched home, probably a lot quicker than they had departed. There was general rejoicing that husbands, sons, brothers and friends had all returned alive and well. Mary was greatly relieved. She could not show her concern so much outwardly as she felt it inwardly, and the one name never mentioned in that household was John Clare. The former school friend, of Mary's own age, Jane Wells, provided the answer to the one question that Mary could not ask of any of her family.

Jane was the only daughter of the village blacksmith, Adam Wells and his wife Prudence. Mrs Wells' sister lived in the village of Barnack, and had been very ill, and so they had been on a visit to help. Returning to Glinton late in the evening, the roads being deserted, the wagon approached a small wood and they heard the sounds of a violin playing, and distinctly through the trees could be seen firelight. Intrigued, Adam brought the cart to a stop and all three descended and, quietly and discreetly, crept into the wood to get a better look. They saw a gypsy encampment, two men dancing with two women, a blazing fire, and by its light the violinist, playing extremely well and obviously enjoying himself. Jane gasped, 'It be John Clare!'

'Who?' asked her mother.

'We was at school together,' whispered Jane. The family crept back the way they came, boarded the cart and set off at a smart pace.

'School didn't do much for him, if all he does is go after gypos,' said Prudence. 'Where do 'e come from then Jane?'

'Helpstone,' she replied.

A few days later, Jane met Ann Joyce in the village and she related the tale to her. Amazed, Ann returned home to tell her family. Mary looked shocked, but at least nothing had happened to him. 'Maybe army life turned his head,' said Mrs Joyce.

'Very like,' said her husband. 'Supposed to be so clever, then consorts with them thieving lying vagrants.'

''Tis a lesson to be learned,' returned his wife. 'Stick to honest work and only associate with decent folks and you cannot go wrong in life.'

Mary sat silently and took it all in. What on earth had possessed John to act the way he did? She could not, with her upbringing, fully comprehend his motives and actions. Then the thought came to her, had he actually joined himself to the gypsies? Was he going to travel around with them the rest of his life? What about his parents and his sister? And finally, had the gypsies taught him to play the fiddle?

But now wedding preparations were first and foremost, and speculation about a person of no consequence to any of them was put aside. Joe and Ann were to be married early in the New Year. It would be a winter wedding, Ann fancied something a bit different instead of a traditional June wedding, and it would take place in late February or early March, depending on the dresses being got ready, not to mention any changes that she had requested in her forthcoming capacity as the new Mrs Clark of Clark's farm, Maxey. It was a big step in her life but she knew that she had trust in the reliable Ruth to help her get settled in. And then Ruth might find a suitable husband and it would then be Ann's turn to help her.

No expense had been spared. The alterations and refurbishment to the Clark's farmhouse had been carried out to the complete satisfaction of its new mistress. The wedding was arranged, the bride and her bridesmaid, Mary, were attired in white gowns and they looked like a pair of snowdrops. All eyes were on them as they carefully walked down the aisle of Glinton church that day. Ann was the bride but Mary was the beauty, and just about everyone remarked on it.

Joseph and Ann Clark were soon ensconced in Maxey. Mary's eldest brother James had not as yet found a life's partner but was taking on more and more responsibilities of running the Joyce's Farm from their father, and William was keeping his eyes open for a farm of his own – whether near or far did not matter providing the price did not exceed his father's budget.

SEVEN

Two years passed and apart from the birth of a son to Joseph and Ann Clark, and the passing of the seasons, there was not a great deal happening in Mary's life. At this point in time her beauty was outstanding. She was as lovely as the most perfect rose before it becomes fully open. The village swains all stood in awe of her, and there were many who would dearly have loved to pay court to her, but she had a type of shy reserve, though certainly not aloofness, about her, since she was polite and pleasant to all parties. She did not seem interested in any males of Glinton, or any of the quite eligible young men that her parents from time to time managed to introduce to her. Mary seemed quite oblivious of any attention paid her and remained the daughter of the house, helping her mother in any capacity she could. She would sometimes drive herself in the family's pony cart or even walk over to see her sister at Maxey to see how all fared. The men working in the field would gaze after her and smile at each other knowingly, and if any were near the road she would acknowledge with a wave of her hand or a 'Good Day' and a sweet smile.

One Sunday, it being a lovely fine dry early summer day, she had been over to Maxey and was returning home on foot, and had decided to make a slight detour by way of the village of Etton. This was a very pretty hamlet and looking to her right she could see the spire of Helpstone church. It was a most unusual style, she decided, but she kept to her path and passed onto a bridle path across the meadows. As she turned a corner of a fence the bright sun almost blinded her, she was obliged to stop and shade her eyes with her hand, and there beneath a tree she saw a man sitting on the ground and using the crown of his hat as a type of desk, and writing with a pencil on sheet of blank paper. The man looked up to see who had interrupted him. There was a visible start from both parties, since he was John Clare! Mary confusedly blushed.

'Mary – it is you is it not?' he asked.

'Yes,' murmured Mary.

'You out walking on your own?' he enquired.

'I am just returning home. I have been to see my sister who now lives at Maxey. She married Joe Clark and they have a baby son.'

'I did not know your sister was married, I keeps to myself and Helpstone. Besides, I was in the Militia a time, and working away from home doing various jobs to earn a crust.'

'So you still live at Helpstone with your parents?'

'Yes I does.'

So he had not gone to be a gypsy after all.

'And how be your parents and the farm?'

'We are all quite well, at the moment, I thank you,' she said. 'But I must be getting back, I see that your are writing.'

'Oh, 'tis nothing, I just kicks 'em out of the clods,' and he laughed.

'Well, good day John.'

'I often come here on a Sunday, if it be dry and fine, I looks for wild flowers or write as the fancy takes me.'

Mary almost opened her mouth to ask what he was writing, but she stopped herself. If he had wanted her to know he would have told her.

'Maybe you come this way from Maxey again?'

'Maybe. Goodbye.' she walked on fairly quickly now.

For two Sundays after that it rained hard. The next Sunday her mother did not feel well and her father insisted that Mary attend church with him. The following Sunday was fine and she decided to go and see Ann and the baby. 'Mind you attend Maxey Church with Ann,' said her father. But Mary, Ann and Joseph had other ideas. Joe and his father were not keen on going to church, especially so since the demise of Mrs Clark, so the Clark family unlike the Joyces only attended two or three times a year. James Joyce would have been mortified had he found out, but as Ann said to Mary, 'We have had enough sermons and hymn singing to last us a lifetime . . .' and Mary felt the same.

So she set out early, and passed a pleasant enough day with the family. She got on well with old Mr Clark and Ruth, and all were sorry when the time came to depart.

'I shall accompany you if you wish,' said Joe.

'That is kind, Joe, but it is light and fine and I am a quick walker,' she replied hastily. Farewells said, she set off to follow the same paths, and there he was again.

'Oh Mary, Mary, I am so pleased!' be began. 'I was feared you would not pass this way again, and it be a month since we met.'

'The weather of course prevented it, also my mother has been indisposed but has, I am thankful to say, recovered her health.'

'Then I too am glad for you,' he smiled. 'What do you do with yourself all day then, Mary?'

'I have my appointed tasks, and I need to learn to be a good housewife when the time comes.'

'You be not courting, them?'

'Not as yet. But I shall know who is right, when the time comes.' She blushed. John Clare gave a slight tremble. There were so many thoughts going on in his brain, and it did make him rather tongue-tied. They walked on slowly and in silence. She glanced at him from the corner of her eye and took in how poorly and shabbily dressed he was, and not all that clean looking either. His clothes made such a contrast to his face, for he was quite handsome, and almost aristocratic looking from his profile, pale skin and bright chestnut hair. If he were well dressed he would most certainly pass for a gentleman. But that was the rub. He was not. He owned nothing. Money, land, property, they were everything in life. You cannot live on fresh air, as both her parents constantly said, and unless there was a miracle and he came into a vast fortune, they would never, in a million years, accept John Clare as a son-in-law. Mary's mind told her all this but in her heart there was the longing, and this man of all she had met had some indefinable attraction that others had not. They said their goodbyes and parted. Two or three more times they met, not always in the same place, once, quite by chance on a little bridge over a brook, which was most pleasant, it being a hot day but shaded by mature trees, and the sound of the water rushing by was relaxing to them both. In previous encounters he had been slightly more confident in his approach to her, but now she felt that she needed to know just what his prospects and expectations were. And so she began quite casually to draw him out. He told her how he had refused to be apprentice to either a shoemaker or stonemason, but had always had varied jobs as a farm worker, or gardener, since he had been employed for a time in the gardens of Burghley House at Stamford. That did impress her. But lately he had walked to Newark to seek work and was now on the point of going to Great Casterton to try his hand at being a lime-burner.

'But, if that does not suit you, then what will?' asked Mary.

John looked sheepish. 'I always was a "shilly-shally" sort of boy,' he replied. 'Well, I suppose, it will by any kind of farm labouring work as I can gets.' He did not say anything about his great ambition, to becoming a published poet.

'How can you keep yourself, and if you marry, a wife and children?' She questioned.

There was a long pause. He could not answer. Finally he said, 'Are you walking out with anyone, Mary?'

'Me, no I am not, and when I do, it must be someone who can provide me with a good home as I have been used to all my life, and of course I must love and trust my husband entirely.'

They walked a short way in silence. There was not a word he could utter in his own defence.

'I must go back now John, I wish you all success in the future. Farewell!' and she walked swiftly away. She did not look back, but had she done so, she would have seen a dejected John Clare standing where she had left him, with tears running down his face. He had failed. She was lost completely and utterly to him. And so Mary continued on to Glinton, to the normal, safe, comfortable existence she had enjoyed so far all her life long.

Some months after this final encounter with John Clare, Mary's brother William acquired a small farm that he could manage, but at a considerable distance to the south of Peterborough, at a tiny village called Coates. It was all of a day's journey there and back, providing one started early in the pony cart, but Mary and her mother found it a most enjoyable change of scenery after Glinton. A year or two after that, William courted and married the vicar's daughter, one Elizabeth Drummond. So followed great rejoicing, but this was marred by the fact that old Mr Clark, following his return to Maxey, had a stroke, and in the space of ten days was dead and buried besides his beloved wife in Maxey churchyard.

Elizabeth and William settled down to married life, and she proved, due to her upbringing, an excellent housekeeper and wife. A year later Ann Clark gave birth to a daughter. With all this family activity Mary was kept busy. Her brother James was running the farm almost without the help of his father, who now had taken a back seat, and had given his eldest son full power to alter and do as he pleased.

In the spring of 1820, Mary had taken the pony trap to Stamford for a few purchases for the family in general. While there she invariably took the opportunity of venturing into the largest booksellers in the town to see what new titles they had in stock. She stood at the shelves surveying the narrow spines of the volumes, when she heard the shopkeeper say to a customer 'Certainly, Madam, this is the new volume of poetry by Mr Clare of Helpstone, selling very well in London, by all accounts, and getting well known in these, his native parts!' The woman purchased a copy and left. Mary stood rooted to the spot; she could not believe her ears. Finally she walked up to the counter and asked what new volumes of poetry they had in stock. 'Why Madam, I have just sold one to the last customer, this is by Mr John Clare, it is called *Poems of Rural Life and Scenery*. The gentleman resides not far from here at Helpstone.'

'I will take a copy,' said Mary.

Her hands trembled so much she dropped her money all on the floor and the shopkeeper helped her pick it up.

'Are you quite well Madam?' he enquired.

'Yes I thank you,' she replied.

The small volume was placed in the trap with the other purchases and off she drove.

Long before she arrived in sight of Glinton. she drove down a little frequented side lane, stopped the horse and took out the book. It took some belief that this work of poetry could have been written by that cottager's son with whom she had gone to school all those years ago, but it was so. She skimmed through the introduction by the publisher John Taylor, and that was all the proof needed. She would not tell her family of her purchase, it would be secreted in her bedroom and read in private. And so she retired early to bed on the pretext of feeling weary. Out came the volume for a thorough perusal.

She was amazed at the variety and quality of the verses. The shopkeeper was right, it was a great success in London. Four thousand copies sold that first year. An established poet, John Keats, only sold one thousand of his book during the self same period. Mary loved the description of nature, of the seasons, and then came a shock. Mary came across a poem entitled 'To a Cold Beauty insensible of love.' The girl was called Eliza, but did he in fact mean Mary? Then the following poem was called 'Patty'. Who on earth was Patty? Not a real name surely? And then, 'Patty of the Vale'! Mary felt two things. The first was the ring of truth in all the poems and the second was jealousy. Jealousy for this unknown girl with this outlandish name of Patty. She lay awake in bed most of the night just thinking. There was no one in the vicinity with such a name as that. She must find out, but how, without rousing any suspicions?

Then the though came to her, what about Jane Wells, who knew many people due to her father's profession as Blacksmith. Maybe she knew of a young woman with that name. With her mind firmly made up, she had an encounter with Jane near the smithy. After the usual polite enquiries after the family's health, she broached the subject. 'Jane, you may think this odd, but have you or your family heard of a young woman around these parts, that goes by the name of Patty?'

Jane thought for a while. 'Mary, I can't say I have. You know not her surname?'

'No, I wish I did,' replied Mary. 'It would make things simpler.'

'Why do you wish to know?' asked Jane.

Mary smiled, 'I cannot say at the moment, but it has to do with something I read!' and further than that she would not be drawn out. Jane promised to keep her ears open, especially as she would soon to making another journey to Barnack to see her aunt. This took place about a month later, and not forgetting her promise, she asked her aunt and family if there was a girl resident anywhere near known as Patty. With that her cousin Susan spoke up. She had heard it said, for it was all the talk of Barnack as far as Stamford, that a young farm labourer, by the name of Clare, had just published a book of poems and no sooner was it out, then he went and got married! He had named her 'Patty' himself, but, she had heard, her real name was 'Martha', and they had been married at Great Casterton, near Stamford, and that the new Mrs Clare was with child already!

Jane's mouth fell open. Never in all her life she had heard a tale like it. A young man called Clare! Surely it would not be the John Clare of Helpstone?

'Yes' said Susan, 'that be his full name. and 'tis said that be where he abides.'

'I wish I had some money as I could go and buy this book, then,' said Jane.

Her Aunt spoke up. 'Susan will get you a copy when next she goes to Stamford. I shall pay for it, as a small gift to you for all your kindness to me.'

'Oh Aunt. I do thank thee,' said Jane, 'but an old school friend of mine asked me if I know a "Patty" and I said I would try and find out, that was all, don't, I beg, go wasting your money on books for me. I shall save, and if I see a copy, I can get it myself, if I've a mind to.'

'Very well,' said her Aunt, 'but if you change your mind, I am willing to purchase it for you.'

Jane returned to Glinton, fairly bursting with her news. The following morning she called at the Joyce's Farm. Mary was writing a letter to her brother William when Lizzie Bird showed Jane into the parlour. The servant closed the door, but instead of returning to the kitchen, as Mrs Joyce had gone out to visit a sick friend she knelt down and applied her ear to the keyhole.

'Oh Mary, I have such a tale to tell!' began Jane. 'That girl Patty whose real name is Martha, is the wife of the youth John Clare of Helpstone! The same boy as we went to school with!'

Mary sat with her mouth open. She changed colour several times, and clasped her hands beneath the table so as Jane could not see how she was trembling.

'And that's not all! They say she is with child already, and that he has gone and wrote a book and it's published and selling in Stamford!! Well, Mary, you could have knocked me down with a feather, yesterday, when my cousin Susan told me.' Mary could not speak, she sat with her head slightly moving in total disbelief. But reason told her it must be true, for had not she purchased a copy of the poems, and were not they locked inside her writing desk? The same desk that was between them on the table on which she was composing a letter.

'Be you alright Mary? You look so strange, I shall get you a glass of water.' So without waiting for a reply, she turned, threw open the door and fell flat on her face over the crouching form of Lizzie Bird. 'You stupid creature! What be you think you are doing?' shouted Jane. 'Fancy a servant eavesdropping, 'tis nothing to do with you, I could have broken my neck, I shall tell your master and mistress!'

'Oh, Miss Jane, I did not mean to, I dropped a pin and was looking for it,' lied Lizzie.

Mary stood in the doorway. 'Please fetch two glasses of water, now!'

'Yes, Miss Mary.'

Jane returned to the parlour, leaving the door wide open, they sat at the table and Lizzie brought in a tray with two glasses of water, deposited it on the table and fled back to the kitchen. The two friends sat and quietly drank the cold water.

'Jane, you are perfectly sure of all this?' asked Mary.

'Well, my cousin say it be all the talk of the villages, in their area, and she has always been as truthful and accurate as the day is long, and my Aunt even offered to buy me a copy of his book, but I said no, I would soonest save for it myself, if I've a mind to.'

They sat a while longer without either speaking, then Mary said, 'That woman, Lizzie, has been here with us a very long time, and I do not want her to lose this employment. Please do not speak of her actions to my parents, providing that you are not hurt in any way, and I shall keep a close eye on her, and should she transgress further, then my parents shall be informed.'

'As you say then Mary, so be it,' said Jane.

They walked a while in the flower garden, before Jane returned home. Mary for her part could not confide to her friend that she had a copy of the poems in question, and it was a good thing she did not, she reflected, or that nosy Lizzie Bird would also have the same information to blab to all and sundry, and that would never do. She did not want to be debarred from any more book purchases by her parents, especially if the former object of her affections were to follow up his success with another volume.

EIGHT

It was not long before the news spread from Helpstone to Glinton, and all details were correct, and that summer the new Mrs Clare gave birth to a daughter, who the excited villagers were told, they named Anna.

'I do bet they don't ever send her here to the vestry School, when she's older!' said Mrs Joyce. Mary felt a great pang of pain and regret inside her. He was lost to her, a married man with a child! A published writer, a poet, who would ever have thought it, it was like something out of a romantic novel, like Mrs Radcliffe's *Udolpho*, without all the dark horror. The vicar of Glinton was intrigued by a local poet, who had been called 'The English Burns' and he and one or two other residents of Glinton had purchased copies of John Clare's poems, and had been deeply impressed with their quality and descriptive powers. Now news soon followed that the new poet had been sent for to go to London to meet and stay with his publishers, and that – wonder of all wonders! – he had had his portrait painted by a well known London artist, called Hilton.

No one in Glinton had ever had that done, not even any members of the Joyce family, either in this present 19th Century or the last. Although from time to time, so-called travelling artists had called at well-to-do houses in the area, including the Joyce's Farm, in the hopes of securing a commission to paint a group or pair, or individual portraits. It was an extravagance that no member of the Joyce family had ever contemplated undergoing. Farmer James was deeply opposed to such sinful vanity as he put it. Mary and her mother were thrilled by the thought of being thus immortalised in paint by even an amateur, but could and would never express the wish to do so and so incur James' wrath.

Gradually, the excitement died down and village life returned to its normal humdrum ways. Mrs Ann Clark had another baby, and then Ruth Clark announced her engagement to the son of a well-to-do Stamford shopkeeper. So that stirred things up in the Joyce family. Mary was cold and distant with the servant, Lizzie Bird, and this was noticed by her mother, who asked Mary if anything was amiss.

'I do not trust that woman. She is an interfering nosey busybody, and I feel that I would not keep her on were I the sole mistress of this house.'

Mrs Joyce was shocked. 'Tell me what she had done,' but Mary would not be drawn further on this painful subject.

Mary still expected, as all did, to make a very good marriage, she had youth on her side and she was still very beautiful. But she never travelled all that far, to meet people of her own social standing with whom she could make acquaintance, thereby finding a suitable bachelor for the purpose. So she languished at home, and the servant was extremely subdued and wary of her, keeping out of her way and having as little conversation as possible. After all, should the unthinkable happen to Mrs Joyce, then Mary would be sole mistress of the farm, unless young Mr James took a bride, but James was so wrapped up in his work that he allocated very little time to himself in his search for a wife; there was certainly no young woman that he fancied in Glinton. He would have to look much further afield to find his heart's desire. So much depended on a suitable union, for there had never been a divorce or separation, except of course, by death, in the Joyce family, and he certainly did not want to spoil the record of the pages of the old bible, going back many generations.

At times Mrs Joyce would almost drive her husband mad by complaining and wishing that these two most eligible offspring of theirs could find suitable life partners, so providing future heirs for the farm. Mary, she conceded, was somewhat reserved, or was that just a bit shy? James on the other hand was a most forthright, outspoken young man, who did not beat about the bush if a thing displeased him, it had to be done to his exacting standards. Mary's great pleasure now lay in walking by herself, with the secret book of poems in her pocket, across deserted meadows in the summer and speaking and memorising the verses out loud. It was a freedom of expression that could not ever be achieved at home, and it gave vent to her much repressed feelings. She did not try to bring up the subject of John Clare with Jane Wells, unless Jane herself had heard some fresh anecdote concerning his life and well being, for instance that Patty was pregnant for the second time. So the poems must have taken off, and he must be making an income from them. Would there be further volumes? The only way was to enquire at the Stamford booksellers, when next she travelled there. She did not want to write to the publishers direct, in case John heard of her enquiry through them, and that would never do, especially as she lived in such close proximity to him.

And so some time elapsed before anything of note was required for the farm and Mary set off to Stamford. Having made for the booksellers, not finding anything to her taste on the shelves, and being alone except for the owner, she broached the subject of a second volume. The man replied that he had heard that a fresh one was in preparation, but he could not tell just when it would appear. At least that was something. It was just a question of time and being patient.

Mary did have quite a long wait. In the meantime, her brother James met a young lady named Lydia Belton, a miller's daughter of quite some miles distant. He pursued her for some months, and then proposed, only to be rejected in favour of another suitor who had of course been kept secret. This was a substantial blow to both James and his family and his mother especially was quite distraught, and the name of Lydia Belton was never again mentioned in the Joyce household. Mary was very sad for her brother but that was fate. Besides, if Lydia had in the course of time become mistress of the Farm, what would have become of her, if they had not got along together, since it was increasingly obvious that she was doomed to spinsterhood.

It was now 1821, and Mary had made several trips into Stamford. The book was indeed in production, but no date had been set for the publication.

Towards the end of October, it being a splendid Autumn day, bright sun on the red and yellow leaves, fresh and clear, she set off for items her mother needed and as before, but not expecting any good news she entered the bookseller's shop.

'Yes. Madam, we have Mr Clare's new volume in stock!'

She looked at the title: *The Village Minstrel*. What an original title, she thought.

'I have not had the time myself to peruse it,' said the shop man, 'but it has had very good reviews in London, and they say it is infinitely superior to his first.'

Mary delightedly paid and left the shop. As before she stopped in the little deserted lane to inspect her purchase. She got quite a shock, for there was a frontispiece, an engraving of a portrait of John Clare himself. painted by a Mr William Hilton of London! What a bonus! Now she could look on his face whenever she felt the need to.

She was in high spirits on her return and her mother noticed. 'Are you alright Mary? You seemed a bit flushed.'

'I have had a very pleasing journey, the sun was lovely and the leaves are so colourful, I felt quite uplifted,' returned Mary, and Mrs Joyce was satisfied. She hid the new book in her writing box, but managed to read a few pages before going to sleep that night. These books were the only real luxury that she had and they were prized beyond even her best clothes and bonnets. Over the coming week, when there was time, and a fine dry day, Mary would saunter off down the field with her new volume concealed about her for a quiet read. She often wondered if she would ever meet John Clare again, face to face. But, it seemed, this was not to be. And it would only have caused embarrassment on both sides. And so she read on and enjoyed this new work, and she was of the opinion that it was much better than the first. 'He has really found his feet,' she said to herself.

NINE

The vicar of Glinton sat in Farmer Joyce's parlour discussing the parish with his friend and churchwarden, and as Mary entered the room the vicar was saying to her father, 'These works are quite exceptional James! We are indeed blessed to have a real celebrity living so close to hand. Why, in London he is hailed as the English Burns! And to think that he was educated at our own vestry school, here, in Glinton. The joy of it makes my heart glad, do you not feel the same, James?'

Mr Joyce rubbed his hands on his legs and thought. He could not reply for a while, there were so many thoughts going on in his brain. 'I am not keen on poetry as some are. I like the songs and hymns I have grown up with. But if a man is pleased to write and makes a success of it, well, then, and gives much pleasure to so very many, it be no bad thing.'

'Well said, James,' returned the vicar. 'I have been over to Deeping, being the nearest bookseller's shop, and I purchased copies of both Mr Clare's volumes. The quality of the verses, subject matters, descriptions of nature are quite enthralling. I am all for having the village schoolchildren learn some of the simpler pieces, as part of their education.' He turned his attention to Mary, 'Good afternoon Mary, I was just talking to your father about the farm worker in the next village, who is a published poet, a Mr John Clare.'

'Good afternoon Sir,' returned Mary sitting down.

'Do you read much?' enquired the parson.

'I am very fond of Thomson's *The Seasons*, also Mr Bloomfield the Suffolk poet. I read *The Farmer's Boy*, but I like much better his *Rural Tales* I think, 1802, if my memory serves me correctly.'

'Well in that case, I can thoroughly recommend *The Village Minstrel*, just published by Mr Clare. It is superior to his first volume of last year, for I have purchased and perused both at my leisure.'

'Mary has her allowance, and I have never imposed any restriction in her taste for reading,' said James. 'She may buy the books if she has a mind to, I cannot be fairer than that.' Mary blushed slightly. At least he had said in front of a witness that he did not object to her owning them. But she would not enlighten the family that she already had them!

The vicar was turning to James Snr again. 'Mr Clare is a frequent visitor so they say to Lord Milton at Milton Hall, and I am also told, to the Marquess of Exeter at Burghley House, at Stamford!'

James' mouth dropped open in astonishment. To think that small skinny boy from Mary's childhood had come so far. 'Bless my soul' was all he could say. The man had far greater social connections that he could ever attain, even if he lived to be the age of Methuselah.

'And these great personages are also patrons to him,' continued the vicar. At this point Mrs Joyce herself entered the room and offered tea to the parson, who respectfully declined as he had other calls to make, and took his leave of the family.

Mary was full of satisfaction; nothing could have pleased her more than to hear of her old companion's rise to the heights that he had attained. Farmer Joyce secretly felt a type of smothered jealousy, but soon brushed it aside. He was a man of property and means with money in his pocket, that meant more to him than some upstart labourer writing popular verses for the aristocracy. Fame of this kind was often short-lived, and fashion was a fickle fellow, a thing to be despised rather than emulated. And in a sense he was right.

The winter came on, and it was a hard one, dark, bitter cold days, the roads and lanes were blocked with snow, then mud. Mary made one or two attempts to go and see her sister Ann at Maxey, but was forced to turn back. It was not until early April did she manage to make the journey successfully.

The sisters were overjoyed to see each other after so many months, the children had grown, and there was a lot of gossip and news to catch up on. Who was courting who, who was married, who was dead, they talked for hours. Then Ann mentioned John Clare and his publications. Yes, said Mary, she knew of it. It was all the talk of Helpstone and Maxey. People had left off talking to him as they feared he might put them in a book!

'How stupid' said Mary. 'Why are folks so silly and superstitious, the man is only making a living by other means than labouring.'

'I wish,' she continued, 'that I too had a talent and could do something, this existence is so mundane, running a home, and doing the book work for Father. I wish I had the ability to draw pictures or paint or play an instrument. Why even John Clare can play the violin!'

'How on earth to do you know that?' asked Ann.

'Jane Wells and her parents saw him playing by a gypsies' fire, while they danced.'

'Good God, he does that, then goes to London and mixes with the gentry! What a life of contrasts! I can barely believe it.'

'Well, she made a point of coming to tell me and that woman Lizzie stuck her ear to the keyhole, having a good listen, and Jane opened the door and fell over her!'

Ann screamed with laughter, at the picture conjured up.

'Serves the nosey creature right. The trouble is she has been there so long for Mother, it is difficult to get a person who is a good cook and servant in general.'

'And honestly and discretion are everything,' returned Mary. 'But should anything befall Mother and, if I am still unmarried, then I shall take steps to get a younger more suitable person, someone who I can take to, to live in and take over the cooking and heavy chores.'

'At least you never had the problems with followers. With old Lizzie, no man in his right mind would give her a second glance, and the length of tongue she has, well, such a scold!' And the two sisters shrieked again and woke up the baby.

The year progressed, and in the course of time supplies were needed, so Mary first called at the Deeping bookshop and then in Stamford, but as yet no one could answer her enquiries regarding future poem publications. The owner of the Stamford shop went so far to say that in his opinion the call for poetry was on the wane. All people now seemed to want was romantic novels, even the most famous and established poets were not selling as well as they used to.

He did hope it was a passing phase, for he had so much good poetry sitting on the shelves. Mary did not know it, but she was in for a very long wait indeed for the next John Clare publication.

The summer came, and with it a new addition of the Joyce dynasty. William and his wife started a family, and a little girl was born, and in time-honoured tradition. William persuaded his wife to have her christened 'Mary Ann' in deference to his mother and sister. His wife would have preferred 'Charlotte' or 'Sophia' but gave in to her husband's wishes. Later on that year, on a lovely warm day, they drove over to Glinton to spend the day at Joyce's Farm. The elder Joyces were as proud as peacocks over this child, as it was the first of the grandchildren to bear their family surname. Mary looked at her brother James, and saw in his eyes a look of great sorrow. It was as if a divine being had said to him, 'James, it is your fate not to have a wife and family like your brother William.' Only time and circumstances would decide this issue.

It was not many weeks after this visit that Mary began to get sudden headaches, and also her eyes began to smart. She put it down to the small print of books, also the keeping of the farm's ledgers for her father. The symptoms continued, and her mother persuaded her to consult a doctor, who in turn supplied various powders, which helped to a certain degree, but, of course,were not permanent. The months came and went, the next event on the calendar was the Fair at Market Deeping. It sometimes proved a diversion, but Mary decided not to go to this one, but would simply stay at home, and she thought privately to keep an eye on that Lizzie woman. An hour or so after the family set off, Mary left her room, and stealthily made her way to the kitchen door. She could hear no sound of any activity, so she looked in and noticed the door at the far end leading to the cellar steps stood open, and silently making her way there, she stood and looked down the steep flight of stairs. There in the dim light of a candle, sat Lizzie on an old stool sampling the contents of her father's barrels. Mary did not want a scene with the woman, especially as there were no witnesses, so back she stole and sat by the fire in the parlour until the family arrived home. In all that time she did not try to summon Lizzie. She thought 'No, I now have this against her, for future reference, and if she is still there when my parents return, well, so much the better!'

Eventually the parlour door opened and Lizzie entered with fuel to make up the fire. She gave a start when she realised Mary was sitting by the window gazing out. 'Beg pardon Miss Mary, I came to see to the fire.'

Mary could smell the alcohol on the woman's breath. 'Very well, Lizzie, make it up then,' she said, and the servant did so and got out of the room as fast as possible.

'So,' thought Mary, 'not had enough this time to intoxicate herself, unless it has been going on for some time, unknown to any of us, and she is quite hardened to it.' It was impossible to say. The family returned, having dropped off Ann and her family at Maxey, and all had enjoyed themselves. So Mary held her peace and waited to see if her parents would in the course of time catch their servant out. Mrs Joyce presented her daughter with a set of embroidered handkerchiefs and her father gave her a set of pencils, for her writing box. Mary was pleased with these simple but useful gifts.

In October the village blacksmith informed Farmer Joyce of an outbreak of thefts in the near vicinity, reported to him from various sources, and as there was a gypsy encampment in the woods near Helpstone, the finger of suspicion pointed in that direction. Glinton boasted some fine properties, with well-heeled inhabitants with desirable possessions. Everyone was vigilant. The Joyce's always had loaded weapons to hand, in the gun cabinet, plus several ancient swords and horse whips.

On the night of 31st October, it being All Hallows Eve, there was so much superstition in rural areas in those days that all honest folks shut themselves in their homes at dusk, and no one ventured out. In the early hours of the morning, James junior woke with a start. He had had a strange mixed up dream, and as he lay in bed trying to make sense of it, he saw a faint light travel across the bedroom ceiling. Someone was creeping across the yard in the direction of the barn and carrying a lantern, which had caused the sudden unearthly movement. He was out of bed and pulling on his clothes, but reflected, in time, that there was probably more than one trespasser, so he crept into his parents' room, pulled back the curtains of the old four poster, on his father's side, and shook the old man's shoulder. There was a grunt and a start and old James was awake. 'Intruders!' said his son. The old man was out of bed in a trice and pulling on a few garments, then the old man snatching a loaded gun and the son a horsewhip, they quietly unbolted the kitchen door, and sneaked across the yard. The barn door was only slightly ajar and a faint light could be seen. Flinging the door open, old James had his gun to his shoulder, in the act of firing. 'Now Then!' yelled his son. Two young male gypsies with a sack each and the lantern had been taking whatever foodstuffs or items had come to hand. They dropped the sacks , not expecting this to happen, as so far, with all their other thefts, they had got away with it. But this was their undoing. One shouted something in an unintelligible tongue, and the other, in English, 'Don't Shoot!'

'You thieving varmints,' yelled old Joyce, 'after my goods and produce, it's the magistrate for you!' The light was so poor, that one gypsy inadvertently knocked his arm against a pitchfork standing up against the wall and so knocking it that it fell, and the sharp prongs caught Farmer Joyce's shirt-covered shoulder, causing him to scream out in pain, and in this quick movement the gun went off in a loud explosion, the bullet just missing the gypsy's ear. Young James lashed out with the horsewhip and did not stop until he had drawn blood on both men, and they took those scars to their graves.

The sound of the gun and the yells had awakened all the occupants of The Farm, and near neighbours also, and a small crowd had by now gathered. Old Joyce lay on the ground with blood seeping through his shirt, the intruders were cowering in a corner with James, whip in hand. One of the neighbours had the gypsies' hands and feet tied securely with rope, another had gone for a doctor. Mrs Joyce had boiled water and was cleaning her husband's blood as it appeared. The blacksmith took the criminals in his cart to a brick outhouse with bars at the window, until they could be taken to the lock-up at the front of the Exeter Arms at Helpstone, for the court was held in a back room of the inn.

There was no more sleep for the occupants of Joyce's Farm that night. It was the talk of the village for weeks to come.

James was quite the hero of the hour, and even the parson preached a sermon concerning crime, and publicly thanked James for helping the whole village from these vagabonds and pilferers. Mary, needless to say, was greatly shaken by all events, but in the course of time her father recovered, and things returned to normal.

Naturally, both father and son were required to give evidence at Helpstone. Neither Mrs Joyce nor Mary wished to attend, so the two Jameses went in the carriage with the other neighbours who had taken part, as they were also witnesses to the events. It was an open and shut case – the verdict: Transportation. On leaving the building, the Joyces saw a crowd of gypsies in the Church Lane and as they got into their carriage for the drive home, one hideous old hag stopped in front of the horses, and screamed out in cracked and rasping voice, 'I curse you and all your family, and be well assured that any man who takes a wife to bed, will not live to make children!'

The horses snorted and set off without the help of the occupants. The old gypsy was obliged to jump clear, but they heard her shouting, and James looked back to see her waving a bony clenched fist. 'Take no notice lad,' were the first words Mr Joyce spoke to his son, 'if they be so clever, why do they beg, steal and cheat honest folks?' His son could only agree, but he felt such a chill go through his whole body when the impact of the old woman's words sunk in. They told Mrs Joyce and Mary all that had transpired that day, but well away out of earshot of the servant, in an effort to stop local gossip.

37

TEN

It was now 1824, and one lovely September day, Mary was walking slowly home from one of her walks, from the village of Northborough along the main road towards Glinton, when she saw a vast cloud of dust kicked up by a long train of wagons and horses. She stood on the grass at the side of the road and watched it all pass by.

There were caravans, but not gypsy ones, for they were very well kept and clean and all painted one colour, but with so much dust it was difficult to say whether they were white, cream or beige. Then she saw the lettering on one vehicle: 'Tussaud's Waxworks'. On returning home she informed the family of what she had seen. Mr Joyce looked up from his newspaper.

'Yes Mary, there has been this exhibition at the theatre in Peterborough, and now they will open shortly in the Assembly Rooms in Stamford. It is the very famous Madame Tussaud herself who models the famous from life, in wax, and puts them on show for all to see. I did see it advertised, but I thought you and your mother and James would prefer to go to Stamford to see it, rather than Peterborough. That theatre is so small and cramped, we don't want to be subject to any pickpockets, and besides, Stamford and the Assembly Rooms are more to your liking, I know.'

The family were greatly taken with the idea of so novel an outing, possibly they would never again have the chance, since the show was always travelling, and travel, in any case, was a slow process. Some ten days later they set aside a day and went over to Stamford. The Assembly Rooms were crowded but well lit, with a small orchestra playing popular melodies and light classical pieces of the day. The Joyce family, like millions before and since, were quite taken aback by the reality of the waxworks. There stood the poet Lord Byron, modelled in 1812, when he rose to fame. Sadly he had in fact died earlier that year. His private life had been one terrible scandal after another, but so many found his life and poetry fascinating. Also the French writer, Voltaire, with long flowing hair, smiling broadly, as if at some joke; Napoleon Bonaparte, looking downwards beneath his famous hat; the Duke of Wellington, stern faced, with his famous pair of boots; a superb tableau representing the coronation of the present Monarch George IV; the American Benjamin Franklin; then Mary noticed the real thing. Seated at a small table with a number of admirers in conversation was Madame Tussaud herself. Very small, beautifully dressed, very dark brown shrewd penetrating eyes, those eyes that had seen the full horror of the French Revolution. That pair of hands that under threat of the death sentence had again and again taken up freshly guillotined heads to make exact copies in wax. She had been companion to Madame Elizabeth, the sister of King Louis XVI, and had been friends with the King and Queen. Waxworks of Louis and Marie Antoinette were sitting, on high-backed gilt chairs, with their two surviving children, and now sadly out of the group only the daughter remained alive, and badly scarred for life by her terrible experiences.

Then came the monsters who had been responsible for the Revolution. A naked man lying in his bath, with a knife stuck in his chest, turned out to be Marat, murdered by a young woman, Charlotte Corday, and as Mary looked at this exhibit, she read the notice, telling of the event and the date, Saturday 13th July, 1793. This was the actual day that John Clare had been born, here, in England, in Helpstone! The publisher of his first book of poems had printed this date in his introduction, and of course, it had been memorised by Mary Joyce.

'Mary, was not the Queen of France a handsome woman?' said her mother. 'And to think how they treated her and how she ended up! It makes my blood run cold to think of them barbaric Frenchies, that it does!'

Nearby was a small table, and on it a scale working model of the guillotine. Its scale was 3 inches to the foot of the real one that had stood in Paris and done so much terrible work. Quite a crowd had gathered round it, and an assistant was kept busy answering questions and even demonstrating it. Many ladies shrieked and almost swooned at the details of stories he regaled them with, as the slanting steel blade rose and fell.

Suddenly she heard a voice, a man's voice, say, 'Dashed pretty young woman standing there, what, Henry?'

'Most fair indeed Roger, not unlike my Ruth!'

The next thing a hand clasped her arm. 'Mary, why it is you!' and there stood Ruth Clark from Maxey, now Mrs Henry Bellamy of Stamford. A most joyful reunion took place. Ruth introduced her husband, who was part owner of a business with his father, and then turned to a good looking young man, maybe a year or two older than Mary. 'This is Mr Roger Beresford, who was Henry's Best Man at our wedding.'

Mary gasped 'Why did you not let us know you were married, we believed that you were engaged.'

'Well, I am not one for a lot of fuss and dragging people for miles, so we got married here in Stamford and I am perfectly happy with my choice.'

'My dear, we all wish you every happiness,' chimed in Mrs Joyce. 'You may as well please yourself as other people,' and she laughed.

Mr Beresford then enquired of Mr and Mrs Joyce if they had seen the separate exhibition in another room. 'Madame charges 6d extra to see this, but 'tis well worth it, for in it are relics of the recent Revolution in France, but, I must say, not for the squeamish, for the reality of it all is shocking to a degree.'

Totally intrigued by all this the Joyces paid the extra money, after a further promenade of the main exhibition, and entered the separate exhibition. Both Mary and her mother were shocked. There were the death heads of the late King and Queen of France, leaders of the revolution Danton, Robespierre, Fouquier-Tinville, and De Launey (Governor of the Bastille). 'My God,' said Mr Joyce, 'to think that little woman sitting so calmly out there, saw all of this, and what else besides, and then handled them, and made these wax effigies! It is utterly incredible.'

'She must have had nightmares,' returned his son, 'otherwise she must have a constitution made of iron.'

'I think I shall have nightmares tonight now I have seen all this,' exclaimed Mrs Joyce. Mary was dumbstruck. She had never imagined such wickedness and barbarity in a so-called civilised society at the time she first drew breath. 'Let us get away from this,' said Mr Joyce. 'I have seen quite enough.'

'The skill of the woman,' remarked his son. 'It is worth every penny to see it all, however shocking.'

They all agreed on this and returned to the main room to Ruth and Henry, and the newcomer, Mr Beresford. Mary could see out of the corner of her eye he was genuinely taken by her beauty, as were so many of the spectators in those Assembly Rooms. She had never drawn as many admiring glances in all the years of her life as that time and in that place.

Mrs Joyce saw it too – 'If she don't catch a husband out of all this, then she never will,' she thought to herself. Mr Beresford kept very close to Mary and made a few observations to her regarding the superb quality of the exhibits.

Mary decided she needed a good look at this man, so making pretence of looking round the back of a group, she moved away and observed him, as a good looking strong featured person, with rich brown hair, very fashionable fine quality clothes with a gold pocket watch. Ruth's husband on the other hand had as pale a face as his wife, with the same blonde hair.

'Henry,' said Mr Beresford, 'look at these uniforms, are they not superb?'

'I suppose they are,' returned his friend, 'but as you well know, Roger, the military 'ain't my forte!'

What a contrast, thought Mary. Mr Beresford having got into conversation on deep matters with her parents, she wandered off on her own to view as she pleased and listen to the music, for it was a rare treat for such as her to listen to pleasant music expertly played. When she returned to the group, they were ready to depart, and Mrs Joyce was just saying, 'We shall be pleased if you can call on us in the near future Mr Beresford. Remember, it is the Joyce's Farm at Glinton!' Mrs Joyce, it must be said, was a real tryer. She did not want her youngest child, so very lovely as she was, to end up an old maid. This man was the right age, he was genteel and presentable, and he had told both her and James that he was in the wine trade. After all he had been asked to be Best Man at Ruth and Henry's very quiet wedding, and that really did speak volumes.

A week later the gentleman in question rode over from Stamford on his fine horse, with a good bottle of claret and one of brandy (for medicinal purposes!) in his saddlebag, as gifts. He did make a good impression on this first visit, although Mary knew of her mother's wiles, and was somewhat cool and reserved. He politely admired the house and principal rooms, Mrs Joyce's flower garden, a few roses left despite the time of year, the good farmyard and stock. Even her brother James got on well with him, laughing and talking. He had been a friend of Henry Bellamy for quite some years, the family business of the wine trade was several generations old, and obviously most prosperous. A match with such a man and family could only be of the greatest and desirable advantage to both Mary and her family. Mr Beresford had both the parents' approval to pursue his interest in their daughter, and after his cordial departure, having left Mary an hour or so, her mother casually said, 'I think that gentleman would make a good husband. What think you Mary?'

'That depends on who he asks,' she replied.

'Well, surely, my dear, you are the object of his desire, and I have no doubt he will propose in the course of time. I know we all have to get to know each other, but the time is passing and you don't want to be left on the shelf, and end up a bitter old maid, as you will know there are several already in Glinton.'

'I will not marry for the sake of it, and as for being an old maid, well, I think that could be preferable to please oneself than be tied down to some man that you have grown to hate and detest, and then to live a life of utter misery and put on brave face on for the sake of others. No. I will do as I feel and my conscience directs, and do not try to persuade me otherwise, mother.'

Mrs Joyce was well and truly taken aback. 'My child, I only wish for your happiness and security after we are gone. Your father and I could not rest easy in our graves if you were in some trouble and alone.' Mary burst into tears at this and so did her mother.

That night in the four-poster bed Mrs Joyce whispered what had been said to James.

'She has spirit, and she knows her own mind,' said old James. 'We can't force matters. Nature takes its course.'

A few hours later, they were awoken from sleep by shrieks and screams coming from Mary's bedroom. Her mother flew into her – Mary was in a terrible state. She had had a vile nightmare, so horrible and terrible that she awakened herself by her own screaming. She sobbed uncontrollably in her mother's arms, as she had done as a small child when bad dreams haunted her pillow. But she could not tell anyone just what terrified her. Only she knew, and that was kept to herself.

The Dream

It was during the Reign of Terror in Paris during the Revolution. Mary stood in the crowd and watched the executions in a never-ending succession, the blood and gore flowed down a channel dug in the road near her, then she saw Madame Tussaud driving a cart full of baskets containing the freshly fallen victims' heads ready to make wax effigies for her exhibition. The next moment she stood in a tumbril with her hands bound behind her, then was propelled forward and up the steps of the guillotine, and before she was strapped to the plank she looked full in to the executioner's face. It was Roger Beresford laughing at her, then the face changed and she looked at the face of John Clare, and then again Roger Beresford. With a horrible laugh the plank swung down into place, and at that point she let out such a scream that woke herself and the household up.

Later that day she tried to analyse the nightmare. John Clare who she always entertained feelings for, but could not have due to his marriage, and now someone who had just entered her world with such suddenness and who wanted her, but for whom as yet she had no feelings either way. She felt only coldness, he could not charm her . . . well, not yet.

Towards the end of November, Roger reappeared. Mary felt a cold chill right through her whole body when he entered the parlour. After a few pleasantries Mrs Joyce sat for a few minutes then excused herself, leaving her daughter to 'entertain'. Mary was working on a piece of embroidery while it was still a good light. 'May I see what it is you are working on, Miss Mary? I may call you Mary, may I not?'

'Just as you please sir.' It matters not to me, she thought.

He inspected her handiwork. 'Very pretty' was the comment. Mary expected no less. 'How do you pass the day?' he enquired.

'I help as much as possible with the running of this house, since we have only one elderly servant, but I do have a bit of a flower garden and I like to walk in the fields on fine days and read.'

'You read novels?'

'I prefer poetry.'

'Really, well I never, cannot abide verse myself. But who do you prefer out of all these poets?'

'I have read Thomson and Bloomfield, but we have a local poet, a Mr Clare, and I prefer him to any.'

'Clare?'

'Yes, John Clare of Helpstone.'

'Ah yes, I do think I saw a volume for sale at Stamford, some time back. Peasant Poet, don't they call the fellow? I suppose it's all romantic rural stuff.'

'I would call it true to life and nature. The descriptions of the countryside are superb. But romantic, no it is not.'

'Ah, well then. We all differ in our tastes do we not?'

Your taste is not mine, thought Mary. All he thought about was drink and money, getting a wife to provide heirs to inherit his trade business.

'I would be most honoured if you would consent to visiting my home and family,' said he.

'I fear the time of year is not really suitable for social calling. The spring and summer are infinitely more suited than these short dark days. Besides, there is much to prepare for Christmas, and I expect my brother William and his family will be coming to spend some time here with us.'

Roger's face darkened. He felt the affront. He turned and stared into the fire. Mary felt a small surge of triumph. She did not like this man. She felt that it was impossible to, and as for visiting his home and family, well, she could not care less. Why please her parents? She had her own life to lead, they had had theirs, for better or for worse, and that was that. Mary continued to work on her embroidery in complete silence. After some five minutes, the door opened and in walked her brother James. Their mother had been out to find him and he wanted to greet the visitor. So the ice was broken by the pleasantries of James, and Roger, sensing an ally, told him the purpose of the visit.

'Well Mary, of course you can pay a visit. I will drive you over myself!'

Mary's face flushed. 'James! There is much to do! Have you forgotten Jane's wedding?' Jane Wells, after a long courtship had accepted Ned Stockwell's proposal of marriage and was to be married in Glinton Church that very Christmas. Mary was to be a bridesmaid, and Jane would become a farmer's wife, and reside at Barnack.

'Mary, there is time enough for all that, and it will be a most pleasant diversion for a short day. Yes, Roger, we are BOTH pleased to accept!'

So it was settled. After the guest had mounted his horse and ridden away, Mary turned angrily to her brother. 'Why did you interfere? I had said no and I meant no. You have made me look a fool. I do not care for the man or his intentions, and I have no desire to involve myself like this.'

Mrs Joyce chimed in, 'Your beauty will not last forever. This maybe your final chance to secure a husband. What do you want child, a Duke or an Earl or something?'

'NO, I do not. Just someone who I truly love and respect, and I do not include Roger Beresford in that category!' But try as she might there was no gainsaying her family, for they were all set upon this plan. James himself wondered if he might meet with a suitable young lady in the Beresford's circle whom he might marry, and as his mother said, she would be over the moon at that!

The day appointed for the visit was fine but cold, but Mary and James were well wrapped up, and set off at a smart pace for Stamford. The address given turned out to be an impressive stone built town house, with steps up to the front door, an elegant portico and railings, situated in a clean and quiet square of the town. Roger himself took their coats and wraps and preceded them up the dog-leg staircase to the first floor drawing room where he introduced his mother, a fine and imposing woman, and his two sisters, Rose and Georgiana. 'Welcome, Miss Joyce,' said Mrs Beresford, and ushered her to a gilt settee. The two sisters were pleasant looking girls, Rose had rich brown hair as her brother, Georgiana a paler shade of brown. The room was not over furnished, but all was of the best quality and most tasteful. Mary had not seen such a room apart from the assembly rooms where she had seen the wax exhibition. She noticed almost at once how her brother was looking at Miss Rose, and she at him. Tea was brought in by a smart young servant maid, and as Mary thought to herself, that relic of a servant they had, Lizzie Bird, could certainly learn a lot from her, in attitude, deportment and dress. This was the sort of person that she would employ herself, given half a chance.

The contrast between the Joyces' lifestyle and the Beresfords' was considerable, but the more she saw of the home and the family, the more she could not help liking it. The family were quite fond of Ruth and her husband Henry, and visiting each other's homes was a regular occurrence.

'Rose and I are so very pleased that you managed to call this year,' said Georgiana smiling. 'It would have been too long to wait until next summer, and Roger has spoken of you on such terms! We just had to meet you ourselves!'

Mary blushed. 'I must confess, I am not used to visiting strangers, but you have all made myself and James so welcome, that it has been a real pleasure.'

Rose clapped her hands. 'I am delighted, Miss Joyce.'

'Do please, just call me Mary.'

Roger was delighted how both his sisters took to her, and he had also noticed how Rose and James seemed oblivious to all except each other. He sent up a silent prayer, 'May I win Mary, and James have Rose!' But not all things in life work out as conveniently as that. It is too much to ask.

'May I ask, Mrs Beresford, did you attend the wax exhibition?' enquired Mary.

'Yes, indeed we did, my dear, I took both my daughters along, after Roger had described it to us, but I must say, I found it a little daunting to see people so very real, looking as if they were about to move and speak, and to know they were only wax! But without such portraits, we all should be so much poorer, and so much in ignorance of what so many famous people look like.'

'Yes, that is my view entirely,' said Mary, 'and it makes such people, most especially Royalty, far more human than we are accustomed to think of them.'

'You are so right, Miss Mary,' this from Roger who had been listening. Mary turned to look at him, and did not realise until afterwards that she had given him a sweet smile. Mrs Beresford, seeing her look more animated, saw just how lovely this young woman really was, and she wondered why on earth such a person had not been snapped up for a wife. But on reflection, Mary lived in a small village quite some miles between two provincial towns and there was not much social contact, such as balls or concerts, to enable people to meet. And beautiful things, whether people, objects, or buildings were more often than not found in the most out of the way places. To find these things is a real bonus.

On the drive home, James turned to his sister, 'Well, Mary, what are your impressions?'

'I like Mrs Beresford and her daughters, I felt quite at my ease in their home.'

'What did you feel towards Roger?'

'He acts quite gentlemanly towards all around him, the same to servants as family.'

'Yes, I felt that too,' said James.

'And which of the sisters did you prefer?' teased Mary.

James blushed. She knew the answer. 'You are a witch, I swear,' laughed James. 'Rose, of course!' They both laughed loudly at that.

There was a look in Mrs Joyce's eyes when they arrived home. Mary knew that look. Her mother was dying to know all details, and later that evening got Mary on her own to satisfy her curiosity. 'And you should see the House! And an upstairs drawing room, you would love the style and furniture, it is all so elegant!'

'And did you meet Mr Beresford senior?'

'No, he had not returned from the business when we left, but I urged James to go as it was getting dusk.'

'Quite right, we don't want accidents. And the two daughters, Georgiana and Rose, they are nice looking girls?'

'Oh mother! Your mind! Yes they are, and the way I saw James staring at Rose! They made a striking pair!'

Mrs Joyce clapped her hands in glee. 'Oh Mary, do you think that there is hope yet for James?'

'Yes, but remember that Rose has been brought up in a town, and lives differently to us, I am not sure if she would make a farmer's wife.'

'Stranger things have happened,' said her mother.

'Pigs might fly,' thought Mary, but made no comments.

ELEVEN

The approaching marriage of Jane Wells was a good excuse for Mary to spend as much time helping her childhood friend prepare for the big day, and to be away from home, should Mr Beresford take it into his head to ride over on the off chance. Her brother James was becoming more cautious in his attitude to a fresh courtship. He did call on Ruth and Henry to sound out the real situation, and finding nothing as they knew against Miss Rose, he went and called on the Beresfords, and was most favourably received. He rode home in high good humour. Confiding to Mary, who simply stated what she had said to their mother, James looked dumbfounded. The poor man had been too swept off his feet to consider the pros and cons for a young lady, quite cultured, living in the town, to change lifestyles to become a farmer's wife in a small village. And he had no intention of making a fool of himself a second time.

Jane's wedding day dawned. It wanted a few days before Christmas, and the old church was decked with as much greenery as could be found for the time of year. Since they had been friends as little girls they had pledged to be bridesmaids for each other, and Mary had kept her promise. The bridesmaid's gown she had worn at Ann's wedding was slightly altered and with a few extra decorations it looked like a different dress. Jane was dressed in a deep cream gown. She was of a very slight build, quite short of stature, with very dark brown hair, and sparkling dark eyes. Her husband was about two years older than her, a fair haired quiet man of sober disposition, and, thought Mary, Jane might settle down and become less talkative, like her husband, and become a caring and loving wife. The church was quite packed, with families of both parties plus all the friends and neighbours. When the ceremony was over, and all the congregation trooped out into the churchyard, it being a bright fine day, no one seemed to want to disperse to the Joyces' barn, where Farmer James and his wife had installed a pair of long tables with a top table for the wedding feast.

Suddenly Mary's attention was drawn to the sound of horse's hooves on the causeway, and looking in that direction and shading her eyes with her hand, as the sun was quite low at this time of the year in the fens, she saw a man slowly riding up to the low wall of the churchyard. He scanned the population, most of whom were starring at him also, being so well dressed and fashionable, and the horse a real beauty, and when he spotted Mary, raised his hat in greeting and flashed a white smile of good teeth. Mary wished that she were miles away, for this was Roger Beresford, who, finding out what the Joyce family was engaged upon, had decided to call on a surprise visit. Dismounting, and leaving his mare to crop the grass at the roadside, he waited for Mr and Mrs Joyce to emerge from the group, bowed, shook hands, saluted the bride and groom, who were also intrigued by the visitor, then he took Mary's hand.

'How do you do? Miss Mary, may I say how lovely you look,' he said quietly. Mary blushed, then turned white as her dress, for many had now witnessed that she was obviously the object of his impromptu call. He had no embarrassment himself and had no thought for what he was causing Mary.

'My dear Sir, we are pleased to see thee,' said her father. 'Pray join the celebrations at the feast in our barn for Mr and Mrs Stockman's nuptials, they will not mind an extra guest, for we are pleased to have thee with us this day.'

'Thank you, but I will not intrude on such a large party. I came to bring a gift of a bottle of wine for your Christmas, which I left with your servant at the house, and to ask after you all.'

'We are all in good health, I thank you,' said Mrs Joyce. 'You are most welcome to the party, you could sit by Mary if you wish!' Mary gave her mother a look.

'No, I thank you again for the invitation, but I must return directly, and I trust, will be welcome to call on you in the New Year?'

'By all means,' said Mr Joyce. 'We shall be glad of your company. Many thanks for the wine, our sincere regards to your family.'

They began to leave. Mary, duty bound, did a small curtsey, but Roger after bowing to her said, 'Miss Mary, you could not be more beautiful if you had been today's bride! And I cannot wait to see you as one!' Smiling, he mounted his mare and rode slowly down the street and out of sight.

After the speeches and feasting, Jane, all agog, came to ask Mary who the fine gentleman was, 'For I am sure, as I said to my dear Ned, I shall soon be doing for you, as you did for me today!' and she laughed and clapped her hands in great delight.

'Jane, stop it! You are such a tease and a chatterbox. Please say nothing to anybody, and if any ask you, say you know nothing, because I don't either!' Mary knew that Jane would tell Ned, but that did not matter, he was the soul of discretion.

Mr Beresford was the only blot on Mary's day. All had passed off wonderfully well. Jane and Ned had had the perfect start to married life, and her parents had done them proud with the barn reception. And so, the feasting over, the speeches and the toasts duly drunk, the newlyweds departed for the smallholding at Barnack, to begin, as all hoped, a long, happy and prosperous life.

The next thing it was Christmas again. The Joyce family had their quiet celebrations mostly with the church services, and a few needful gifts exchanged hands. The New Year came: 1825. Mary felt the loss of her friend Jane, there was a fall of snow, so it would be rather a hazardous undertaking to try and call until the spring came again. The snow was also providential in stopping James from going to Stamford in pursuit of Rose, and her brother doing the same to Mary. At least she could read her poems and dream, and think of what might have been. She had not heard any news concerning John Clare or his family, and it would be some time before she could get into Market Deeping or Stamford to make enquiries as to a new publication. But for those with leisure and money, the novel was all in all. Poetry, she well knew, had now declined in favour with the reading public. Mrs Joyce was at times visibly fretful. She wanted the fine days of Spring and to see a happy outcome of all her hopes and aspirations regarding James and Mary. Mary dreaded the approach of fine weather. For herself, she would be strong enough to firmly decline a proposal of marriage, but this business of James and Rose nagged at her constantly. The lifestyle was not compatible to a young town lady, and she did not want Roger for a brother-in-law, any more than she did for a husband.

The open countryside was her paradise, the wildlife, the birds, the old farm, the workers she had known for so many years, and to be uprooted from all this and be stuck like a doll in an elegant doll's town house was just intolerable to her. She now knew that with all its attendant hardships, life as the wife of John Clare, in a little cottage, would have been far more suitable to her nature and temperament than she had ever though possible when constantly being told that she was a lady, who should marry a gentlemen, and live in fine style. It did not always bring happiness.

Eventually, news arrived via her sister Ann that Ruth was pregnant. This was a great upsurge of spirits and excitement in the farm household. The birth was expected in August, and Ann was already making her own plans to help the Bellamys in any way that she was able, for she truly loved Ruth as her own sister.

Georgiana Beresford had managed to obtain a set of the latest fashion plates from London, and was making a careful study of them, seated by a good fire in her parents' drawing room. Having made a choice, she now enlisted the help of her mother to extract enough cash from her father for the purchase of some very fine pale green silk and other trimmings, to be expertly made by the best seamstress that Stamford could boast for the forthcoming 'season', in the hopes of attracting the eye of a future husband. One gentleman in particular, Mr James Joyce junior, who had begun to pursue her sister Rose! Yes, this girl was prepared to go to any lengths in order to get him for herself. 'Well,' she said to herself, 'all's fair in love and war!' And if she could not 'catch' James, well, she might get a bigger and better fish in her net. The fabric was purchased, the seamstress commissioned to produce the garments as per the design, and in the space of two weeks, the job was completed. The combination of the new gown with her light brown hair, dressed in the latest style, made the transformation complete. She was stunning. Even her mother marvelled at her daughter's taste. The effect needed a male but not of her family, to see just what the reaction would be, and she did not have to wait long. It so happened that her mother and Rose were called away without warning, due to the illness of Mrs Beresford's sister in the nearby County of Rutland. Georgiana did not wish to go, and so feigned a headache.

As soon as they departed in the carriage, she changed into her new gown and was standing admiring herself in the cheval mirror in her bedroom, and wondering if there was anything else that could be added to improve her general appearance, when she heard the sound of the front door knocker in the hall below. It flashed on her that it must be James! Quickly she left the room and was descending the staircase as the servant girl was opening the front door to the visitor.

'Oh Mr Joyce, I am sorry but Mrs Beresford and Miss Rose are away from home today,' said the servant, and James would have turned and departed had not Georgiana from her vantage point on the stairs called out, 'Mr James! Pray do come in! I am at home as you can see!' James did see. He stared in amazement, she looked so very lovely, fresh, youthful, her green gown so sweet, it set off her complexion and hair to perfection. He stared, then said, 'Good day, Georgiana,' and gave a little bow; she had now reached the hall and gave a curtsey.

'Please be so kind as to accompany me to the drawing room, and I may offer you some refreshment? Tea?'

'Thank you,' said James quietly. He was quite taken aback at the change in this young lady.

'Jenny, please to serve tea, thank you.' She led the way and they were soon seated on matching sofas on either side of the marble fireplace, with a Pembroke table dividing them. Jenny soon appeared with the apparatus of tea things. James tried to converse.

'Your Aunt is ill, then?'

'Yes, we do not know the nature of the complaint, but I hope it is not infectious,' said Georgiana. 'I trust all your family at the farm are well?'

'Oh yes, we are all in good health and spirits. I expect Roger and your father are at the business premises!'

'Oh yes, they will be there for hours yet. And I did not feel disposed to leave home with mother and Rose, and I am so glad that I did not, for then I would have missed you, and you would have had a wasted journey!'

'Well,' said James, 'I do intend also calling on Ruth and Henry, for my sister Mary is most fond of Ruth, especially as now due to her condition.'

'Ah, yes, quite,' returned Georgiana, and smiled knowingly. James, slightly embarrassed, glanced round the now familiar room, and his eye fell on the group oil painting that hung above the card table. It had been painted by a competent artist some five or six years previous, and showed Mr and Mrs Beresford with Roger, Rose and a very young Georgiana. Comparing the painted image with the elegant and fashionably dressed young lady who sat directly in front of him was something of a revelation, for Georgiana was certainly more beautiful than her sister, Rose, who seemed almost dowdy by comparison. Before he had realised it, he spoke the one word he was thinking, out loud 'Lovely!'

'Beg pardon?" said Georgiana looking for a moment startled.

James coloured, then quick as a flash, 'The tea, it is lovely!'

'Ah, I am so pleased it is to your taste,' she said.

They sat and drank the tea, and then James in an attempt at conversation asked if she had made any new drawings lately.

'No,' she replied, 'But I have been learning a pleasant piece of music by the late Mozart, and I enjoy playing it to my family.'

'May I also prevail on you to play it for me?' asked James.

'It will be my pleasure,' and she rose and walked over to the harpsichord, and then played brilliantly 'The Turkish Rondo'. James had never before heard this piece. He knew the name of Herr Mozart but not much else, and he was quite entranced by the lovely tune. In quite a trance, he stayed rather longer than he would have done under the normal circumstances of just calling on Mrs Beresford, for the opportunity of being in the presence of Rose. When he finally departed it was dusk, and no time left to call on Ruth and Henry. It was quite dark when he rode his horse into the farm stables.

TWELVE

In bed that night he thought over the day's events. He had seen Georgiana in a different light. Her looks and style and talents had quite charmed him. His mind and feelings were all in a quandary. So he decided to confide in his sister, Mary, the first opportunity he could get to discuss things in total privacy, without being overheard by anyone. The next morning, breakfast being over, Mary was halfway up the stairs to fetch some needlework, when James ran up and touched her arm. 'Come with me, please, I want your opinion.' They continued up to the landing, then James opened the door at the end leading to the attic cum servants' bedrooms, only one of which was occupied by Elizabeth Bird. He opened the door of one of these disused rooms, they entered and he closed the door.

'James, what on earth has got into you?' asked Mary.

'You know I went to Stamford yesterday?'

'Yes, and I know why, to see Rose!'

'Exactly, but both Rose and her mother were out, there was only the servant girl and Georgiana there.'

'Well, why did you stay so long, then? Did you go and see Ruth and Henry?'

'No, there was not time. I just visited with Georgiana.'

'Well, I do not think that was quite proper,' said Mary.

'She offered me tea, she seemed more adult, she had on the most lovely dress and she looked so very beautiful. I could not say no.'

Mary laughed. 'You will tell me next that she is the object of your affection!'

'That is it in a nutshell,' said James.

Mary gasped and sat down on an old chair. 'But you have been so taken with Rose, and she with you, right from when you first met.'

'Yes, I know, I do so wish I was not so confused with my feelings. If only Rose had been at home, but her Aunt is ill and she and her mother had gone into Rutland to see what could be done.'

There was a long pause, then Mary said, 'I know you have wanted a wife, now, for a long time, and you have been disappointed once, but surely you can see that these are town girls, and, I fear that neither would be quite suitable for a farmer's wife, any more than I feel I can adapt to becoming a wine merchant's wife.'

James stared. He had not fully considered all the implications. Had he married the Millers' daughter, that would have been more suitable, the union of two country people on the same level, but now he saw the Beresford girls in a fresh light, and he could better understand Mary's feelings towards Roger.

Mary continued, 'I know Roger wants to marry me, at least, he thinks he does, but if he asks I shall refuse. I do not like him at all. We all know he is good looking, wealthy, he would provide me with all, and more, than I could reasonably ask for in life, but I do not and I cannot love him as a husband. Mother and Father want to see me settled with a husband, the same as they want a wife for you, but it is no use marrying for the sake of it and then regretting it for the remainder of your days on earth.'

Another long pause. James sank onto an ottoman. 'Mary, you are so right.'

'Let us go down now, in case we are needed,' said Mary. 'We both have our decisions to make, but at least you know mine.' So they left the attic room and descended the stairs to do their own tasks. They thought they were unobserved, but the majority of the conversation had been overheard by the servant who had crept up to her own room to make the bed and heard voices, and had stopped to listen at the keyhole. She now knew just how the land lay!

'That Miss Mary!' she said to herself. 'She must think she is better than anybody else, with all her advice and preaching! All she is going to be is an old maid, like me, and one day she will live to regret it!'

Some ten days or so passed, then a letter arrived address to Mary. Ruth had written to tell her that that Mrs Gibbs, the elder sister of Mrs Beresford, had died of cholera, and that on the arrival of Rose and her mother, the doctor had warned both of the great danger. Rose, being young and strong, and always very fond of her Aunt had packed her mother off home to Stamford, and she, meanwhile, had insisted that she stay and help with the nursing. But with all the help that money could buy it was of no avail. The funeral had taken place, and the very worst news was that Rose herself was taken ill. None of the family dared to go and take charge of matters, it was left to the doctor and his professional nurses to try and pull Rose through. Ruth promised to write again, as soon as she had further news.

Mary was indeed upset. She liked Rose, and then to impart the news to James! She managed to get him alone in the fields and it was a good thing she did, for he broke down completely. Mary had never seen a grown man in the state her brother was. It was a long time before she could persuade him to return to the house to hear the hopeful and comforting words of his parents. Rose had youth on her side, surely she would not succumb like Mrs Gibbs had done?

More than two weeks passed, and not a word. The family were growing desperate, then a letter arrived from Ruth for Mary. It was the very worst. Poor Rose had died. Her family were totally grief stricken. The body had been sealed in lead before being placed in the coffin, which had been taken direct from Rutland to the family church in Stamford to lie in state for one night, to avoid being in the home. The funeral was over and done, and Rose had been buried in the little burial ground of St Martins-Without, Stamford.

There was no work done that day by any of the Joyces. Mary quite thought her brother would go mad. Now she was gone, he had fully realised that it was her he loved and not Georgiana, and he did not want a substitute. Mr Joyce, as head of the household, wrote a long letter of condolence to the Beresfords. Mary corresponded with Ruth, it was the only pleasure she had at this time. Visiting was out of the question, due to the winter and bad roads, and the abject gloom and misery never seemed to end. Life seemed an endless nightmare, and her headaches returned tenfold. There were times she feared also for her sight, and was obliged to lay aside her beloved needlework, or Clare poems.

In the spring, Mary persuaded her mother to take on a young girl to help with the washing and chores, and learn from the now long employed Elizabeth Bird. So, one of the farm workers' daughters, one Sally Tibbles, was finally selected. She was a good choice, Mary and her mother liked her, she was cheerful and hard working, and Mary know she would, in time, become a far better employee than old Lizzie was now. Lizzie was at times grateful for help, and at other times resentful to have to be pleasant and teach the girl about the household duties that were expected of her, but then, that is a common case with elderly women (and men) who are forced, out of necessity, to educate youth to take their place.

The year wore on. There had not been any visiting done by any of the parties to or from Glinton or Stamford. It almost seemed a too embarrassing situation, where none could pluck up the courage to make the first move. Midsummer came and went. It was hot and dry, the roads thick with dust. Early in July, James took the decision to ride over to Stamford, he had the idea that he wanted to see the spot where Rose was buried, and also to call on Ruth and Henry, as it would so shortly be Ruth's confinement time. He was reluctant when the moment came to use the knocker on the front door of the Beresford home, but use it he had to. He hardly dared speak when the servant showed him into the presence of Mrs Beresford, who was of course attired in deep mourning. Roger and his father were at the wine merchants, and then poor Mrs Beresford broke down in a great flood of tears. She had so hoped that this young man would have been her son-in-law, but it was not to be. Tea was sent for, and with it came Georgiana, white faced, also in the deepest mourning. Her eyes were red rimmed, for she wept daily for her beloved sister, and when James requested if she could possibly accompany him to the burial ground to view the spot, since it was not possible until the New Year that a headstone be placed in perpetuity to mark the place, Georgiana readily agreed, and the pair set off.

It was no great distance, and they hardly exchanged a word going, as so many people of the Beresfords' acquaintance bowed or nodded to Georgiana as they passed. It was obvious to James what deep regard and respect the family were held in. They reached the small cemetery and Georgiana pointed to the mound under which her sister lay. James sank to his knees in grief, and Georgiana walked away to hide her feelings also, in the pretence of reading the existing stones. Finally he got to his feet. 'Thank you, Georgiana. I shall not forget this kindness. Next year at this time, I shall come again and see the memorial.'

They returned to the house and he took leave of mother and daughter, and then rode off to call on Ruth, whom he found in great health, and looking forward to the impending birth. He stayed a while, then Henry came in from the shop and was most pleased he had called, after so long an absence. Finally he said his farewells and rode out of Stamford.

He was nearing Northborough, when black clouds covered the sun and a great crash of thunder sounded overhead, his horse was so startled it reared up on its hind legs, and James was obliged to dismount and try to lead the animal by the bridle. The thunder rolled again and the heavens opened in the most violent downpour he had seen for a long while. He was getting soaked, the horse stopped in its tracks and would not budge an inch. They were a few yards short of the gateway leading to the courtyard of Northborough Castle, or Manor House as some called it, and he decided to make a run for it, seeing as there were two men already sheltering from the storm. Thinking that his horse would follow him in due course, he let go the bridle and took to his heels in flight. He was almost at the entrance when the loudest peal of thunder sounded, and a great zigzag of lightening flashed from the skies. That was his last moment on earth. He was struck and killed outright. The men ran to his aid but all was in vain. The owner of the Castle had his body carried in, and instantly recognised who it was, the horse was then caught and taken to the stables, until someone could call at Glinton with the appalling news.

The cries and screams of Mrs Joyce could be heard at a considerable distance, farm workers and neighbours alike took to their heels and ran, thinking the good lady was being murdered. Mary lay on the floor in a dead faint. Mr Joyce collapsed in the fields when one of his men went to tell him and take him home. James' body was brought back that evening in a cart filled with clean straw. One of the workers was despatched to Maxey and another to Coates. Then Ann Clark would have to write to Ruth, who would inform the Beresfords. The entire village of Glinton was plunged into grief and mourning. Young Mr James was well liked, kind, fair and polite to all. He would have made a worthy successor to his father.

It was decided to start a fresh row of Joyce graves in the churchyard. James was buried on the south side of the church, not many yards from the porch, by the side of the main path. Mary spoke privately to the vicar that she wanted the next plot for herself when the time came, irrespective of who passed on next. The vicar made a note; the promise was indeed kept in the future. The church was packed. The doors left open for the remainder of the villagers to hear the service and join in the hymns, for the whole of the village closed down that day, and all attended out of liking and respect. Henry Bellamy drove in his carriage with his friend Roger Beresford as companion from Stamford. The families of Maxey and Coates came, and it was decided, by William, that he would sell his Coates farm and take over the running of the Joyce's Farm, in James' stead. With the crush of people and the sad circumstances, Roger could not speak at all to Mary, but she noticed him looking at her at every opportunity he got. At last, they were all left to their shared grief when, friends and neighbours having departed, a type of peace settled like a dark grey blanket on the family.

THIRTEEN

It took quite some time for William to find a purchaser for his farm. He had worked hard over the years to build it up, putting the house in good order, complete with a good stock of animals, to make a pleasant, warm dry dwelling in which to live and bring up a family This space of time gave Mrs Joyce and Mary the opportunity to re-arrange their home to suit both William and his wife and child, and have fresh duties to occupy their minds. But Mary never knew until now just how much she had loved and missed James, and for Mrs Joyce, it was very hard, for James had been the first child of her body.

But then a letter arrived from Henry Bellamy, telling of the birth of a son to Ruth, and both were doing well. 'I hope Ruth never has to go through what I have had to be put through, and suffer the loss,' said Mrs Joyce, when Mary read the letter aloud to her.

'No,' said Mary, 'and I for my part have no desire to marry and have children!' and she left her mother open mouthed, and went for a solitary walk in the meadows.

It was now late August hot and dry. She made quite a contrast in her black clothes and bonnet against all the greenery and poppies. Then she heard the sound of a horse's hooves, and there coming down the road was Roger Beresford! 'Oh my God,' she thought, 'where can I hide?' but there was nowhere in that flat landscape, and in any case, at the height he was, and her in that awful black, she stood out like a sore thumb.

'Good day, Miss Mary,' he called, and dismounting, tied his horse to a nearby gatepost and entered the field, bowing as he did so. 'I have called with some happy news for you and your parents,' he began. 'My good friend Henry tells me that he now has a fine and healthy son!'

'Yes, we do know thank you,' returned Mary. 'We have had a letter.'

'Ah well, it has still not been a wasted journey, for I longed to see and speak to you again, and had it not been for all the sad and recent happenings to both our families, I would have said before to you what I would like to say today.'

'Pray, Sir, I am not in need of conversation, I am out for a short walk, we are so plunged into grief and gloom, it cheers me slightly to walk in the sunshine, my obvious regret being my dear late brother cannot enjoy it also, as you, no doubt, feel the same for poor Rose.'

'Miss Mary, you sum up everything so very well, in a nutshell and always to the point. Yes, of course, I do understand and I do feel the same as you, but Mary, life must go on, and I have come today to tell you how much I respect and love you, and to ask you to be my wife!'

Mary's face went scarlet. 'Please, do not ask such a thing of me sir, we are both in mourning, there is a time and a place for all things, but this is not it!'

'Mary, my lovely, there is no better time than the present!' and with that he threw his arms around her and held her in a vice-like grip and kissed her passionately on the lips. Gasping, she struggled to free herself, but he tried to hold her ever tighter. She got one arm free and tried to push him away, but now he had one leg wrapped behind one of hers, and out of desperation, she clawed his face and made it bleed. The shock and pain finally made him desist, and gasping and sobbing, she turned and ran as hard as she could, reaching the farm parlour. She collapsed in a chair. The servant girl, Sally, was polishing, and looked up in alarm. 'What is the matter Miss? Shall I fetch you a drink?'

'Please do, Sally.'

Sally sped to the kitchen, nearly knocking down Mrs Joyce. 'What's the matter, girl?'

'Mary!' answered Sally.

Mary gulped down the water and her mother could see that something was very wrong. 'Well,' asked Mrs Joyce, after Sally had left the room, 'what is the trouble now?'

Mary carefully related all that had happened and everything said.

Mrs Joyce was amazed. 'But he wants to marry you!'

'A gentleman would not have forced himself on me in such a fashion, for me to have to fight him off!' returned Mary. 'And should he dare to show his face here, you do not admit him! I would not marry that man for all the tea in China!'

Mrs Joyce said nothing. There was really nothing that she could say. To argue with her daughter any further was pointless. So she gave up, and continued to try and work out her feelings and emotions on the changes required in the house, for her remaining son, his wife and child.

Eventually a buyer was found for William's farm at Coates. He bought almost all of the furniture and fittings, since to try and move such items a long distance was hazardous; things could so easily get broken. As it was, his former home had all and more than he had managed to purchase originally. Elizabeth, or as many now called her, 'Mrs William' was delighted with her new and most commodious home. She was polite, pleasant and easy going, and got on well with all around her. The same could not be said at the moment of her daughter, Mary Ann, who took a very long time to settle in. She missed her birth-home, the familiar landscape, the little friends she had made with the Coates village children, for Coates was a very small place in those days compared to Glinton, a large and prosperous village, with spacious stone-built houses, pretty gardens and orchards, and a much prettier countryside. The move took place at the very beginning of December, so Mary Ann did have Christmas to look forward to with her grandparents and Aunt Mary.

And so into the New Year of 1826, Mary had decided to keep well away from Stamford, unless she was with other people. Never again on her own. So William and his wife now shopped for supplies in Stamford, and little Mary Ann enjoyed the treat of going there immensely. Mary herself occasionally went on her own as far as the Market Deeping bookshop, and on one occasion enquired of the shopkeeper if he knew of any new publications appertaining to Mr John Clare, of Helpstone. Yes, the man replied, there was a new volume in preparation, and had been for some considerable time, but when it would come out, or what the title would be, he did not know. During the summer, she, her sister Ann and her husband Joe and the children did all manage to get to Stamford in order to see Ruth and Henry, and the baby boy, who had been christened George Clark Bellamy. The whole day was spent with them, there was much to talk over, scandals, gossip, and of course, Mary confided the details concerning Roger and his violent proposal. Ruth had heard from reliable sources that the amorous gentleman was now actively pursuing an heiress at Oakham, and had been at the chase for some time! Mary was so very much relieved to hear that. She felt that a great weight had been taken away that had been crushing her both bodily and spiritually, but now, thank God, she was free.

The first anniversary of James' death came round, and for no apparent reasons, she had the most terrible headaches, her eyes smarted and sometimes her vision seemed impaired. Then as suddenly as it came, she was back to something like normality. She did not confide to the family just how ill she felt on these attacks, it would have caused grave concern to all.

With her sister-in-law now resident. there was more time for herself, the simple pursuits of wandering at will the quiet green lanes, the flower-filled meadows, and she even several times drove herself over to Barnack to see how her old friend Jane was doing, and to find out any further news or gossip concerning John Clare. Martha, or 'Patty' as he called her, seemed to be constantly pregnant.

He had been to London to stay at his publishers several times while his wife had to be at home and struggled hard to look after the children and also his ageing parents. It was certainly not at all fair. The man had respite from labours but the wife had none, and the burden was getting bigger and heavier for her to bear.

Mary felt justifiably outraged. She would most certainly sympathise with poor Patty's lot, and she herself, despite her feelings for the poet, would not like to be treated like that by him, had she married him, either. Jane was the one person that she ever spoke to regarding the poet, his life, or works. It would never do to mention him to her mother, for fear of any suggestion of attachment or reason why she refused to marry Roger Beresford.

There was now a little companion in the excursions to the meadows, in the form of her niece Mary Ann. With her mother and grandmother occupied in the house, the little girl sought the company of her Aunt, much to the pleasure and delight of Mary. It was a novel experience for her to look after a child, since, when she was young and even a lot older, she always had someone else to look after her. Mary Ann soon learned the names of the wild flowers, and which berries were safe to eat and which not. Mary sometimes took a volume of poetry on these rambles, and would read aloud some of the simple verses to the child, who then learnt and repeated them to great effect. The child took especial delight in the birds and the beauty of the various songs. There was something almost indefinable in the simple joy and satisfaction in teaching her little niece about nature and the countryside, passing on her knowledge as it had been passed on to her, and so on, all down the generations. Mary reflected on this whilst seated on a rug beneath a large oak tree in a meadow about a mile from the farm, watching Mary Ann gambolling about and chasing the butterflies, hoping to catch one, since the child had the fanciful idea that they were really fairies in disguise, and if she could catch one, well, it would grant her a wish!

Mary herself chuckled with delight at the child's fantasies and decided that next time when she went to Peterborough or Deeping she would obtain some volume of fairy stories to entertain Mary Ann. In due course, supplies were needed, and Mary set off to Peterborough, and after the necessities were packed up, she scrutinised a booksellers to see what could be had. She was unknown in this establishment, and asked to see what volumes were on offer of children's literature. She was shown several quite fine examples complete with illustrations, which, she had hoped, she would find to keep the child occupied on wet days. After making her choice, she then enquired if any new volumes of poetry by Mr Clare of Helpstone had been published recently. There was a negative answer, but, the shopkeeper understood, a new book was shortly to come to press. At that moment, a very finely dressed lady turned from the shelves, and smiled at Mary. In a strong German accent she said, 'How gratifying to find a kindred spirit in this town who admires Mr Clare! Do excuse me, but he is a friend of my husband and myself. Allow me to introduce myself, I am Mrs Marsh. My husband is the Bishop of Peterborough and Mr Clare has been our guest at the Palace on a number of occasions! We simply adore his poetry!'

Mary was indeed taken aback, but remembered to curtsey. 'Good day, Madam, I am pleased to make your acquaintance. I am Miss Joyce of the Joyce's Farm, Glinton; and yes, I admire his verses very much too. I have collected all his published volumes so far.'

'As you live so near Helpstone, maybe you have met Mr Clare?' enquired Mrs Marsh.

Mary blushed, 'I met him in the vestry school at Glinton Church where we were educated. My father is also a church warden besides being a farmer.'

'Oh, that is so excellent,' said Mrs Marsh, 'it is such a pleasure to meet with someone who understands these matters. Do allow me, as I frequent this establishment almost weekly, to write and let you know when the new work comes out. It may only be a matter of months, since it has, I believe, been some years in the preparations.'

'I could not put you to so much trouble,' said Mary. 'I do not often come to this town, I generally use Deeping or Stamford, and I always call in the bookshops there.'

'Miss Joyce, it would give me great pleasure and satisfaction to inform you when the work is out. I think it more likely that this shop may get its copies before Deeping or Stamford does. And, of course, dear John Clare will in all probability call on us with a copy as a gift.'

So Mary gave in and Mrs Marsh wrote down the name and address in case she forgot any details. Mary returned home with her purchases. She kept the book for Mary Ann until the next day as a surprise gift. The child hugged and kissed her many times for such a splendid gift.

Mary casually mentioned to her family that she had met by chance the wife of the Bishop of Peterborough, in the bookshop. All the family were most impressed. None more so than her father, considering his long involvement with Glinton church. He secretly hoped that the Bishop and his wife might invite Mary to the Palace at some point, and that he could then escort her personally himself!

And so the year went along. There were visits to and from Maxey, and a visit to Stamford to see how the baby progressed. And then Mary's sister-in-law, Elizabeth or 'Mrs William' announced that she was pregnant. Oh, they all prayed, let it be a boy, and carry on the Joyce name!

FOURTEEN

Mary had, in many respects, taken her niece under her wing regarding her education in reading and writing. It began to be remarked upon in the village, how fine a little lady Mary was making of her. None noticed it more than the vicar. Chancing to meet Mary on one of her strolls, he mentioned the fact of how well Mary Ann was learning. 'Yes' said Mary, 'I remember all I was taught so well, and I do enjoy imparting my knowledge, however limited, to her.'

'My dear, you are too modest!' said the vicar. 'I have a proposition to put to you. As you are aware, our present schoolmaster is shortly to retire, and I have been unable to secure a suitable replacement But I feel that with your skills, and way with children, you would fit the post most admirably.' Mary's mouth dropped open. What a thought! What a proposition indeed!

'Well' she gasped, 'you have taken me by surprise, and no mistake! I really do not know how to answer you! You must give me time to collect my thoughts and consider!' She walked home very slowly, turning it over and over in her mind.

Playing with Mary Ann, she asked the child if she enjoyed all the learning lessons that she had helped her with. 'Oh yes, Aunt Mary, I really do,' smiled the child. Later that evening after Mary Ann had gone to bed, she told the assembled family of the vicar's offer. Her father was quite horrified. 'What, my daughter, working as a school mistress!' he almost shouted.

'But I have had great success with Mary Ann,' said Mary. William and Elizabeth agreed. Elizabeth said, 'I think it is a splendid idea, father-in-law. Mary will be doing a service for the village, and besides, there is the thought of a small income.' Mrs Joyce, ever practical, agreed whole-heartedly on this point.

'Then I am resolved,' said Mary. 'I shall try it, and see how it goes, for I am not obliged to do the job for life, am I?'

Her father had to back down. He did not want to upset the vicar, and in doing so the village as a whole, and Mary could do with some type of employment since there were two servants, as well as Mrs William and his own Ann. And so Mary, the next morning, knocked on the vicarage door and gave her answer in the affirmative. The vicar was overjoyed. 'My prayers have been answered!' he said.

The schoolmaster was duly notified and Mary attended several classes to get the feel for the job, and to assess the abilities of the various pupils. They were mostly the children of her own father's and now William's farm workers, who soon realised, after the initial shock of finding a school mistress instead of a master, and the ensuing merriment of the situation, that they could not do as they pleased, since the Joyces paid their fathers' wages. Within a few weeks Mary had taken over completely, and the former teacher had left. She drew on the inspiration of her own school days in order to teach, and make lessons more enjoyable and interesting, and she would often gaze at the spot where she and her sister Ann used to sit, and then where John Clare sat, and wonder if another boy would ever turn up who would turn out to be a writer. But as she knew, it was really too much to ask or expect, as genius happens so very rarely. Mary discovered that she had a real flair for teaching. She had more of a purpose in life, and the pupils enjoyed the experience too. In time she found that she was the most popular woman in Glinton. Everyone praised her natural ability and her own parents were justly pleased and content. So the months past, and in the spring of 1827 a letter arrived addressed to Miss Joyce, the Joyce's Farm, Glinton, in a hand that she did not know.

'Oh' she thought, 'Is it from Mrs Marsh?' Yes, it was. Mrs Marsh had kept her promise. The new volume had the title of *The Shepherd's Calendar*, and the Peterborough shopkeeper had reserved a copy for Mary, to be collected at her convenience. A few days later, it being a Saturday, Mary journeyed into Peterborough, and paid for her copy.

She enquired of the shopkeeper if he knew if Mrs Marsh was at home, so that she could thank her in person, but the shop man advised her to call at the Palace, and leave a message if the lady was out. A good idea, thought Mary. Into the Minster precincts, and turned right into the gateway leading into the Bishop's Palace. She rang the bell, a footman answered. Mary asked politely if His Grace the Bishop and his Lady were at home, but they were both out visiting in the parish and he did not know at what hour they would return. So leaving a verbal message of thanks to the good lady, Mary walked back to the pony trap, and set off for Glinton. She decided to write a letter of thanks to Mrs Marsh, in case the footman forgot, so, this done and posted, she then had leisure to peruse the new book.

This work was divided up into the months of the year, rather than the four seasons, which made it all the more versatile and interesting. The more Mary read, the more she realised what a work of art she held in her hand, and, the finest work of John Clare to date. There were passages of such exquisite beauty and truthfulness, she was moved to tears. As she read on the notion came to her to write down page numbers and passages, that she could read aloud to the village schoolchildren, and get them to memorise the more simple direct verses that appertained to the daily lot of their lives and parents. These verses were too good to keep to herself, they deserved the largest possible audience of any generation. It took quite some time to achieve her objective, but finally it was done and she felt satisfied with her labours. During one of her lessons, the vicar paid an impromptu visit to the vestry and sat entranced by what he heard. It was wonderful, it was inspired.

'Miss Mary, what is that book you have been reading from?' he enquired.

She told him. He took the book for a quick perusal. 'It has only just been published,' said Mary.

'Then I must get myself a copy too,' said the vicar, and obtain one he did. So these two residents, at least, of Glinton, both owned the published works of John Clare. The vicar on completing his reading of the book, declared the man to be the finest nature poet that England had produced so far. There was something in every month of the year to touch the heart of any reader. Mary was in total agreement with these sentiments. The vicar was a true soul mate in his love of literature, and of nature in general.

The months passed, and Mrs William gave birth to a son. There was quite a commotion when it came, with regard to agreeing about a name. She would certainly not agree to the baby being named James or William, especially as she had given way in the name of the first child, Mary Ann. No, she was not to be swayed on this matter, but to give her rather religious father-in-law a bit of pleasure, she turned to the bible for inspiration. She chose the name Adam, and Adam Joyce, the child was duly christened. Mary Ann was so pleased to have a baby brother, to help with his everyday needs and to see him grow. Mary herself was happy.

She entirely approved of the break from all the family tradition of those repetitive names.

The new baby prospered and grew, and time passed quite quickly, and then in the Spring of 1828, it being a Monday, Mary opened her school only to discover that there were several children absent. 'There be a fever Miss,' said one boy.

'A fever?' questioned Mary. Then a thought struck her. Her own niece Mary Ann had complained of a headache last Sunday evening, and was at this moment in bed, because she felt unwell. A cold chill went down her spine. The girl had caught something off her friends, the other village schoolchildren. Mary hurried home after school to find that her worst fears were confirmed. The doctor had already been called and had diagnosed scarlet fever. The baby and even Mrs William must not have contact with Mary Ann, so the lot of caring fell to Mrs Joyce herself and the two servants to nurse the child. The little girl's temperature soared and her head ached terribly, then the rash developed, and her throat was so sore and painful, she could only take liquids. Then came the appalling news that two of her friends had died of scarlet fever, and it shook the family, and Mary closed the school for the duration. The doctor attended daily, and did all he could despite the lack of modern day medicines and medical knowledge. Child mortality was always quite high, but the Joyce family had been unusually lucky for a number of generations in not losing any babies or very young children to the Grim Reaper. Poor Mary Ann became worse and worse and finally expired, and the grief of the family was immense.

No one else caught it in the family, and now all attention focused on the baby, Adam. It was some time before the village was declared free of the epidemic, and a lot longer than that before Mary could steel herself to re-open the school. It seemed unthinkable that her beloved niece, whom she almost regarded as her own daughter, the love being so great between them, would never enter the building again, and sit smiling at her, that at times to hide the emotions that suddenly welled up inside of her, she would suddenly leave her chair, and get out into the churchyard. There at the furthest corner, away from the church, the hot tears would stream down her cheeks uncontrollably, and it would be some time before she could control her emotions and return to the class and her teaching duties.

FIFTEEN

The harvest of 1830 had been a good one, and farmer James Joyce was proud of the amount and quality of its produce. It was the day of the traditional harvest supper, held in his farm's barn. His family and workers were even now putting the finishing touches to the decorations and food and drink to be served up to one and all. The weather was superb, and old James being on his own for once decided to look at his fields in the golden sunshine. After walking for some considerable time, he felt a little weary, his age was beginning to take its toll on his ability, so he entered a lush green meadow where a fine oak tree had stood growing some two centuries or so, and he stood resting his back against the trunk. Feeling the need to rest a little more comfortably, he slid to the ground, and sat, enjoying the view between a pair of large roots growing out of the trunk, like a pair of gnarled legs. Gradually, with the sunshine filtering through the leaves, the sound of birds singing, he drifted off to sleep and during his sleep, the old man exchanged this world for the next. His end could not have been more peaceful or happy as his eldest son's had been so violent.

The hours slipped by, and back at the farm, Mrs Joyce was asking William if he knew where his father had gone, since his was the main presence needed to start the proceedings, and greet the workers as his guests at the feast. William and several of his labourers set off in various directions across the fields trying to find a sign of the missing man. Eventually one of the workers in looking over a low hedge saw old James with his eyes closed resting beneath the oak.

'Master, Master,' called the man running up to him, gently shook his shoulder, only to discover the sleeper was a corpse when the body fell over without a sound. William wondered whatever the matter was when he heard old Tom yelling his name at the top of his voice. Running over, he took one look, and knew the worst. Mrs Joyce on being told, collapsed. The feast turned into a type of wake. They took a farm cart with clean straw and laid James' body in it for the short journey home.

With his father's passing, William became one of the head men of Glinton, but he did draw the line at becoming a churchwarden as his father had been. In fact all the family now tended to veer away from that establishment, rather to the dismay of the vicar. Old James' funeral was a large and lavish affair. The village turned out in force for the occasion. It was not without relief for all concerned, especially the widow, when all was over and done, and they could look to themselves and centre all attention on baby Adam, who was their hope for the future.

SIXTEEN

Time passed and they all tried to put their respective sorrows behind them. One Summer day, in June 1832, Mary's sister Ann and the children came over from Maxey to spend the day. The two sisters sat in the old garden enjoying the fine weather and admiring Mary and Elizabeth's efforts at the flowers which they had mainly grown from seed, when Ann said, 'I wonder how John Clare likes his new garden.'

Mary started. 'What do you mean, Ann?'

'Have you not heard? Well, the family have moved from Helpstone and now live at Northborough.' The name of Northborough sent a chill right through Mary's frame. 'Yes,' continued Ann, 'the old cottage where he was born was only old pokey tenements, not healthy or much room for his family, so Lord Milton organised a large cottage with two acres of land for him to rent, and try his hand at farming. I wonder if he will make a go of it. They say the cottage is well set back off the lane, and no near neighbours, so he can farm and write to his heart's content. I should say it's paradise!'

Mary was astounded, 'No, I have heard nothing about him for a very long time. What happened to his parents? Are they still alive?'

'Yes, and they live in the old cottage, so it's a lot better and quieter for them with all those children gone.'

'How many children did they have?' asked Mary.

'I am not too sure on that point,' said Ann, 'maybe seven, but I don't know.'

Then Adam and his cousins came into the garden, and their own personal conversation ceased.

Mary began to wonder just where in Northborough the cottage was placed. She wanted to see it, and curiosity did eventually get the better of her. Early in September of that year, it being a superb day weather wise, she decided to walk across the meadows to Peakirk, and so on into Northborough, also that way, not missing anything on her stroll. Passing a clump of trees on the left hand side of the lane, there stood, extremely well back, in a large front garden, a new detached thatched roof cottage. Walking slowly by, she took in all the details. No door was visible. It must be at the rear, she thought, since there were two chimneys at either side. There were windows overlooking the garden, that had a long driveway on the right hand side of it. One bedroom window only was placed in the centre of the house, and out of the corner of her eye she thought that she saw a movement. 'Probably the curtains in the light breeze,' she thought. Having ascertained as she surmised the actual Clare cottage, none else being anywhere near, she walked on quite quickly, round a bend in the lane, where there was a dense spinney of trees and there was the sound of beautiful bird song issuing from it. Mary thought to herself 'I shall just sneak in there to have a look and see what bird it is.' It was as well she did so. A few seconds later she heard running footsteps coming down the lane, and then a voice, a man's voice, once so familiar to her, and now not heard for years, the voice of none other than John Clare himself, calling, 'Mary, Mary, where are you?'

Then the footsteps stopped. Mary squatted down behind a large bush and peered through the leaves. She knew him at once. His hair had receded, he had filled out and put on weight, but his face was so fine and handsome. She hardly dared to breathe. The little man gazed round and round, he even looked up into the clear blue sky. 'I know I saw you, Mary, I did not dream it, how can you disappear so and how can I forget?' Round and round in a circle he walked, then looking back down the lane towards his home he shouted 'I am coming Patty!' and then he was gone.

Mary waited for some time before she dared to move for fear of him returning. She could not face him. She felt acute embarrassment for the reason of being seen by him from his new cottage window, and he would know it was only from sheer inquisitiveness that she had walked by. Half running, half walking, Mary came past the quaint church and so into the main village, then Northborough Castle loomed up on the left hand side, and she shuddered as she passed over the spot her brother James had been so violently struck down. Then on to the main road over Nine Bridges and on to Glinton. 'I am glad I did not try and bring Adam along,' she thought, and had it not been for the thicket and birdsong, it would have meant a confrontation with him, and that she did not want at any cost. He was a married man with a large family. She adored his poetry, secretly she loved him, but there, that was totally private, no one must ever have an inkling of why she had never married, and had rejected suitors. And there must be vast numbers of women who, down the centuries had harboured smothered desire and passions for men that they could not have, and had died old maids. Mary hurried home, vowing to herself never to set foot in Northborough ever again. Her curiosity had been satisfied. His cottage was pleasantly situated and fairly isolated, with land and space and to be his own man and practise cottage farming, as well as the all important poetry. Surely he could only prosper in such an environment. Mary sincerely hoped so.

A few days later she received a letter from Ruth Bellamy in Stamford. All the family were well and prospering, and relations with the Beresford family had cooled significantly since Roger had taken the heiress for his wife. Her fortune had compensated for her lack of beauty; and now the general rumour was, that he had set up a mistress a few miles off, who he could visit as often as he pleased since there was travel involved with the family trade, thus combining pleasure with business.

Mary was shocked and showed her mother the letter. 'Now do you see, I was right!'

Mrs Joyce had to admit defeat. 'But there is still time, Mary, you still have your looks and who knows? What say you to a widower of your own age with a good sum of money in the bank?'

'Ah, mother! Please! No more of this matrimonial talk or intrigue. I am sick of it!'

So Mrs Joyce just thought to herself, 'Well, we will just wait and see, my girl.'

The wily woman did, in fact, have an eligible widower in mind. When William lived in Coates, he used to pass by a farm at Whittlesea, not far from the famous Whittlesea Mere, a vast stretch of water, the home for many centuries to all the water birds and various aquatic life. The man who owned this farm, a Mr Jacob Hunter, was past forty, a native of Yorkshire, who had married somewhat late in life, and whose wife had died in giving birth to a stillborn baby. The man was of good character, according to William, his home was a reasonable one, and the farm doing quite well. All this he had confided to his mother, who in Mary's absence had always bewailed the fact that her attractive daughter was fast becoming an old maid, with no prospect of being a wife and mother. Elizabeth, 'Mrs William', had met Mr Hunter several times, and siding with her husband and mother-in-law, felt that it would be a good thing if he and Mary hit it off, she being so very good with children, too, she deserved at least one of her own before it was too late; and, as it was, time was running out for Mary, but just how short none of them would ever have believed had they been told.

So, conspiratorially, it was agreed behind Mary's back to invite Mr Hunter over for one Saturday, when he could afford the time, and see his friends in their new home at Glinton. Elizabeth wrote the letter on behalf of her husband and herself, and it was duly sent. About a month passed, when one Saturday morning, Mrs Joyce very casually informed Mary that a visitor was expected that day, but that she did not quite know at what hour. 'What visitor?' queried Mary.

'Oh, a friend that William is acquainted with, from Whittlesea,' she said airily.

'A farmer?'

'Yes.'

'And is he bringing his family too?'

'There is no family.'

Mary smelt a rat. 'And is this man single, mother?'

'Well, you see my dear, his poor wife died.'

'And to what purpose, as if I could not guess the reason for this visit!'

'But he is a friend of both William and Elizabeth, he knew Mary Ann, and, I am sure he will be so pleased to see Adam for the first time!'

'I shall take the pony trap and go and visit either Ann or Ruth, that way, he will not feel obliged to make polite conversation with a total stranger,' and she rose to collect her things and get the pony harnessed.

'No, oh no, please Mary! You must not go! William says he is a good man, and who knows, you both may take to each other. It is my dearest wish, as you know, to see you settled and secure in life. Your poor father wanted it so much, he would lay awake at night and say it so often to me!' and Mrs Joyce began to cry.

'All of you are really too bad, you cannot leave me in peace! I do like my situation being free and single and I do so enjoy doing the teaching, although the print of the books is small and my eyes often hurt, but I feel I am doing some good in the world, and not living a life of idleness and pleasure! And see how right I was about Roger Beresford! I could never take to the man. Just see how he had turned out! He could have taken my money and set this same woman up, at my expense!'

'Yes, my darling, I know,' sobbed Mrs Joyce. 'I wish that I had discussed this before, about Mr Hunter, but he is genuine person, both Elizabeth and William say so, so please, please my darling daughter! Stay and meet him! You will never know what you may be missing unless you meet him for yourself.'

There was really no argument that Mary could say against this final reasoning.

'Very well, but I caution you, do NOT leave me alone with him or suggest me showing the garden, or any such nonsense!' Mrs Joyce humbly promised. Mary was white with fury, and could hardly say a civil word to her brother and sister-in-law.

The upshot was a cold and very restrained atmosphere. Eventually, the sound of wheels announced the arrival of Mr Hunter. William and Elizabeth, carrying Adam in her arms, ventured out into the yard to greet him. Mrs Joyce and Mary sat in the parlour and waited. Mary had taken up her needlework and barely acknowledged the man's words. Her mother nudged her with her feet, and Mary looked up. He was about 45 years old, well built, red faced, hair that had once been black as the raven's wing, but now showed more grey than black. Simply and cleanly dressed, just as a respectable farmer of his years should be. He had a strong Yorkshire accent, and it was obvious that both William and Elizabeth liked him a great deal.

'A fine farm, a fine home!' said he to the assembled company. (Adam had escaped to the kitchen to play with the maid Sally.) 'A reet fine little lad thar has Will! Ee, but I was sorry to hear about the little lass! But then that's life, I lost my Emma, and no chance of another as yet to take her place!' Out of the corner of her eye Mary saw a slight smile on her mother's lips. This was meat and drink to Mrs Joyce. She thrived on it.

'Would you like some tea, Jacob?' asked Elizabeth.

'Aye, I thank thee, I'm reet parched,' said he. So Elizabeth rose and left the room, almost knocking into old Lizzie Bird, who was up to her old tricks of coming for a listen.

'What do you want Lizzie?'

'Only came to save your legs mistress, as I expect the gentleman wants tea or some other refreshments.'

'Yes. Please make tea, thank you Lizzie', and the servant scuttled off.

Over the tea, Mary felt the visitor's gaze directed at her. She had hardly spoken or looked him directly in the face, but he was certainly taking her in. Mary worked on. She was making and embroidering covers for chair backs to save the upholstery. Her work was most tasteful. The centre panel consisted of a classical vase filled with a selection of types of flowers of all colours and hues, to brighten and enhance any room they happened to be displayed in. Mr Hunter half rose from his chair to gain a better view. 'Well' said he, 'My Emma did try to do summat like that there work, she were a decent needlewoman but not to your standard Miss!'

Mary partly smiled and coloured slightly. 'Yes,' said her mother, 'our Mary is most accomplished, she has been doing needlework for many years and she is the teacher in the vestry school as well.'

'Well I be blowed!' exclaimed Jacob. 'Thar never did tell me o' your sister's talents, Will!'

'Mary likes to be busy, and our parson, seeing how good she was with helping Mary Ann, asked her to try her hand at teaching, since the old schoolmaster was leaving us,' said William.

'Mary is so popular with all the village children,' said Elizabeth.

Mary blushed, 'I am sure Mr Hunter is hardly interested in my lowly work. Why don't you show him round the farm, William?'

So William did. Jacob was most impressed with all he saw. 'My God,' said he, 'what a tragedy about James, but then, you would not be master here, and thou cannot compare your old farm to this, can ye?'

'No,' said William, 'I miss my brother and my father terribly, I feel both their presences here at every turn, but as you say, I am now master, and my brother was strong and healthy, and barely two years older than myself, and he was courting, so had he married, it would have been highly unlikely that I would ever have inherited this farm.'

They walked on in silence, then Jacob asked, 'Why is thy sister not wed?'

William shrugged. 'She don't seem to be interested in it. Seems happy as she is – walks, reads, sews, likes being the village schoolmistress. But she did have a follower a while back, son of a Stamford wine merchant. He seemed a good catch as we all thought, but Mary rejected his advances, he took up and married a lady of wealth, and that in turn helped him set up a second wife!'

Jacob burst out laughing. 'You don't say, Will. But there, it just shows ye. Rogues aplenty still abound. Mary's a find looking woman, that she is. And no followers now, then?'

'No, none.' There was a very long silence. Then Jacob made up his mind.

'Dost think Will, would she consider me?' The absolute suddenness really did take William by surprise. His jaw dropped open and he said when he got his breath.

'Are you completely serious Jacob?'

'Aye. lad. Thou knows I miss Emma and I need a replacement. She is a fine lass, a farmer's daughter, a farmer's sister – why should she object to being wed to a farmer? Surely, then, it makes perfect sense. I can provide for her, I have a good house, I am not without means and my Emma had no complaints, why, she had everything she wanted, and more besides.'

'If you do mean it, then I can broach the subject in a day or two, and I will write to you if I think that there is any hope in it for you, and that is the best that I can do for you, Jacob.'

'Ee lad, thou are a true friend,' and Jacob grabbed hold of William's hand and shook it.

SEVENTEEN

It was almost a week before William did approach his sister. He said nothing at all to Elizabeth or his mother. It was none of their affair what Mary chose to do with her life. He liked and respected Jacob Hunter, and he would not mind him for a brother-in-law. His farm was good, his house could always be improved upon, there was money all round that could be spent, and spent well. So he decided to meet Mary out of school and take a stroll in the nearby meadow, it being a fine dry day.

'Is something wrong, has something bad happened?' queried Mary on seeing him standing in the churchyard.

'No, all is well,' he replied. 'But I need to talk to you.' So the two entered the pleasant meadow that was one of Mary's favourite places.

'What did you think of Mr Hunter, Mary?'

'What does it matter what I think, he is your friend, and you are at liberty to ask who you please to the house.'

'Yes, I know that, but that is not the question I asked you.'

'Well, then, he is a plain dressed but clean outspoken man. What more can I say.'

'Do you like him?'

'I neither like nor dislike him, William. What is he to me? Nothing at all.'

'But he could be more if you let him!'

'What do you mean?'

'He wants a wife, that's what, and he has taken a fancy to you.'

'Oh, my God! Whatever next! Did that man ask you to ask me? Did he?'

'Jacob wanted to know if you might ever consider him for a husband, so I promised to let him know if you had a mind to it.'

'Well you can tell him I haven't!' stormed Mary. 'Whatever next. William! I suppose Elizabeth and mother are also in on this one too!'

'No, I do assure you, I have not breathed one word of this matter to either, it is strictly between ourselves and Jacob Hunter.'

Mary stood silently taking deep breaths. She took it all in and was, when she calmed down somewhat, quite sensible of the proposal. It was in a sense flattering that a total stranger should find a single woman of her age still attractive enough to be drawn to, but no. She felt it would never do. There was nothing to charm her about this man. He was just so lonely, and he was catching at straws. Then, a new thought came to her.

'William, how did Mrs Hunter die?' Reluctantly he told her. 'And would you have me go the same way, then!'

'Don't be so silly Mary! Lightning doesn't strike in the same place twice,' and then he realised the full impact of what he had said and Mary burst into tears. It took a while to comfort her and calm her, but at last she said,

'I am very sensible of the advantages of Mr Hunter's offer, I feel he means well, but, no. Mr Hunter had better go and hunt for a wife elsewhere,' and she turned on her heels and began to walk home with a very subdued William trailing behind. William kept his word, and did not divulge Jacob's intentions to either his mother or wife, who both questioned him as to whether there was any interest on his part towards Mary, and his reply was an emphatic 'NO'. And so there the matter ended. Life carried on, the farm, did well, Adam grew and was a healthy active boy, and Mary taught on.

From time to time, Mary would purchase various literary magazines published in London containing reviews of new books, and due to this investment, she built up a small but fine selection of books in her own taste. During the late summer of 1835, she read several reviews of a new volume of poetry called *The Rural Muse*, published by the firm of Whittaker's & Co, priced at seven shillings. The author was John Clare! How her heart leapt up when she read the name. As soon as she could do so, Mary set off for Deeping and purchased a copy. There were illustrations of the Northborough cottage, showing the back with its central door, also another picture of Northborough Church.

The selection and quality of the verses were exceptionally fine, and here and there, a girl was mentioned in one context or another, 'Mary'. Could John have meant her, was he thinking of her when he penned those lovely lines? Mary secretly hoped that it was her, and no other Mary. And if true, then she and she alone had been immortalised by a famous poet. She fairly hugged herself with quiet delight and rapture. *The Rural Muse* was to be the very last book that John Clare would have published in his (and Mary's) lifetime.

At the time of both their births, George III had been King, with his Queen Charlotte, then his son, and heir, had taken over due to his father's bad health, and there had been the Regency period from 1811–1820. When the old King died, his son had become George IV. In 1830 George had died and had been succeeded by his brother, who had become William IV, and now this King of seven years had gone, and his niece, a young girl named Victoria, had succeeded to the throne. The newspapers were full of the events in London, and Mary and her family were totally absorbed in this perusal. The newspaper print was very small, and she strained her already overtaxed eyesight to the limit, and so gave herself some rather bad headaches.

In the August, on a visit to Ann at Maxey, she was shocked speechless when her sister informed her of gossip from her near neighbours and various friends, concerning the well-being of the Clare family at Northborough. The poet had some kind of mental and or physical breakdown. He could not make a go of being a cottage farmer, everything was a complete disaster. The upshot of it all was that he had gone into a private lunatic asylum in or near Epping Forest in Essex!

Poor Mary! She had never felt such pity, such heartfelt sorrow for another human being in all her years on earth. Sitting there, silent and stunned, her sister asked her if she was all right. Mary could only reply after some time, and then with the greatest of efforts, 'You have shocked me, Ann.' How on earth could John Clare have failed, with the advantage of a new large cottage and all that land to do as he liked with? He had a wife and growing family to help, he was not alone. What livestock had he got? Born and bred in a rural community, he knew all there was to know about agriculture in general. It was beyond her comprehension. Finally, she voiced these thoughts to Ann, but Ann knew nothing of the whys and wherefores of this farming fiasco. 'He must have really gone off his head', was all she could come up with.

Mary returned home in the deepest gloom. Obviously, his last book, *The Rural Muse*, had not sold well, so in that case, lack of money and the despair at its failure had brought about this said situation. But poetry sales in general were poor. There was simply not the demand. All the general reading public liked and wanted now were exciting novels. Mary owned a few, but her preference was for poetry, and John Clare's was first on the list. Her mother did not bother with books and nor did her brother, but Elizabeth liked romantic novels, and the odd poem.

The months passed, it was now 1838. There had been much talk for some considerable time as to William taking his wife and son for a holiday to the East Coast, since none of them had seen the sea, and Elizabeth and Adam both wanted this experience. Accordingly, arrangements were made, and at the end of June, they set off in the carriage. Mary and her mother would take care of the farm in their absence, the workers were loyal trustworthy men, employed for long years, who knew their jobs and did them well, so there really was no reason for any concern in this matter, and during their absence things went swimmingly.

On Friday 13th July, Mrs Joyce did not feel well. It may have just been her imagination, or the oppressive heat of the day, but she felt such general unease that she said to Mary, 'I do feel that something is going to happen. Please God, let it be nothing bad.' In the early evening she felt slightly sick and retired to bed early. Mary sat alone doing the farm accounts for William. There came the sound of a plate smashing on the kitchen floor, and a curse from Lizzie Bird. Mary got up to see what was the matter. The old servant was on her own, as Elizabeth had insisted on taking Sally along as well as a general factotum-cum-lady's-maid, and so giving her the chance to see the ocean. Mary entered the kitchen to find Lizzie on her knees picking up the fragments of a willow pattern dinner plate, a great favourite of Mrs Joyce's.

'What are you doing? How did that happen?' demanded Mary. The woman looked up, her eyes bloodshot, and Mary could smell the excessive alcohol on her breath. She had been in the cellar again.

''I'm sorry Miss Mary, it just sort of slipped out o' me hand! Tis Friday 13th, unlucky for some!'

Mary said nothing, but she would tell her mother in the morning about Lizzie's drinking habits. Something more valuable could have been broken. She retired to bed.

About 11.30 p.m. she was awakened by her mother calling her name. She got out of bed, lit a candle and put a lace shawl around her shoulders. She entered her mother's bedroom. 'I am sorry to disturb you my dear, I did call for Lizzie but she must be sound asleep, so I called you.' Yes thought Mary, sleeping off the effects of drink. 'My stomach is rather upset, would you please boil a cup of milk to help my digestion?'

'Yes, of course. I will get it directly.' Down to the kitchen with her candle she went, and lit several more on the table. Taking a small copper pan she poured the milk from a pitcher into it, then poked the fire, but it needed making up, so going to the store room where the wood was kept, she took a bundle of very dry sticks and put them on the fire, and used the bellows to get a good blaze before putting on the milk pan. A thought came to her, Friday 13th, the 13th of July. There was something significant about that date, but what was it. Standing there, she was suddenly transported back to the Assembly Rooms in Stamford in 1824, when the wax exhibition was there, and in her mind's eye, she could see the ghastly face of Marat, as he lay stabbed in his bath, and the date of the murder, Saturday 13th July 1793. 1793! Yes, that was it! It was John Clare's birthday, and that date of 1793 was the actual day of his birth, two miles from where she was standing at Helpstone. 'I wonder how he is and where he is,' she pondered. 'Now let me see, how old does that make him today . . .' so she calculated – he was forty five years old that very day. Softly, she said out loud 'Happy Birthday John Clare, wherever you are, and many of them.'

Standing in the dim light of the vast kitchen, and almost in a dream-like trance, she did not quite realise how close she was standing to the fire. A large shower of sparks erupted from the dry kindling and landed on her night attire, which was composed of cotton and lace, the gown with its puffed sleeves, lace shawl, lace cap and streamers were alight in seconds before she fully realised it, and she became a human torch, screaming as loudly as she could for her mother, then overcome by the agony of the flames she fell to the flagstone floor. Mrs Joyce heard the screams and the crash, and moving as quickly as she was able, got down to the kitchen. The sight that met her eyes in the poorly lit room was horrific, but keeping her wits about her, the old lady emptied a large pitcher of cold water, left standing for the morning, over her daughter's body. The flames went out, the jug was dropped and smashed on the ground and Mrs Joyce was screaming over and over, 'Lizzie, Lizzie! Quick, help, quick!' But there was no help from that quarter, the drunken servant slept on.

Out into the yard she ran screaming, 'Help me, help me!' The Blacksmith's forge was close at hand, and the occupants heard her and ran to see. Old Mr and Mrs Wells and their son who had now taken over from his father helped the poor woman into their home. She collapsed into a chair. All she could cry out was 'Mary, Mary, burnt!' The father and son took to their heels and entered the farm kitchen. There was very little they could do. Mary was barely alive, her burns to the head and face were truly terrible. They went and pulled the servant out of bed and splashed cold water on her to sober her. Lanterns and candles lit, father and son, as gently as they could, carried Mary upstairs and laid her on her bed. Lizzie stayed to keep watch while the old man ran back to his wife, and the son saddled a horse and galloped off to fetch the doctor. Mr Wells found that Mrs Joyce had fainted and his wife was doing her best to revive her. The vicar being a very close friend of the family, Mr Wells ran to knock him up, and down he came to see how matters stood. They all did whatever they could but to no avail. Mary Joyce exchanged time for eternity at about 1.30 a.m. on Saturday 14th July 1838. At sunrise, the doctor set off to Stamford to inform the coroner, and that gentleman set off immediately for Glinton.

He was taken to see the body and then held his court at the scene of death in the kitchen. He questioned all parties to ascertain there had been no foul play, then said to Lizzie Bird, 'Why, Miss Bird, did you not hear the screams of Miss Joyce, or the shouts for help from Mrs Joyce?'

Lizzie hung her head and was silent for a long time.

'Well, I asked you a question and I demand an answer,' thundered the coroner.

'Beg pardon Sir, but I was so very sound asleep,' she began.

'So sound asleep not to hear all this commotion? There is more to it than that, I will be bound,' said he. 'Woman, are you in the habit of imbibing alcohol?' Lizzie hung her head and went crimson. 'Your face tells me all I want to know,' he said. The doctor, Mrs Joyce, and the Wells family glared stonily at her. 'Very well then. To sum up, I shall write Miss Mary Joyce, aged forty one, cause of death, Burnt Accidentally.' And so it was.

The village was stunned by the news. Everyone rallied round, but Mrs Joyce was in control. She told the vicar that the funeral had to take place as soon as possible, due to the terrible state of her poor daughter and the hot weather, and in any case, she wanted it all over and done with before William and his family arrived home.

'You will not write and inform him?' asked the vicar.

'No, I cannot. They were moving about, and even if they were not, I would not dream of spoiling their holiday.'

The vicar said nothing, but fetched the village carpenter to knock up a plain simple coffin, not really finished off in any way. Mary's body could not be laid out due to its state, so a shroud was found, and sewn up so none should look on the once beautiful face, now so badly scarred by fire. Straight after the morning service on Sunday 15th, the grave digger and his assistant set to work with a will to open the hard dry ground on the vacant space next to Mary's brother James' grave. They toiled in the heat of that Sabbath day, their clothes wet with sweat.

The carpenter loaded the coffin on to a cart and took it to the farm. Mary's remains were placed inside and the lid nailed down. Mrs Joyce, on seeing this plain article, was so shocked that she found some faded tapestry bed hangings, and had the carpenter cover the coffin so none could view it. This done, she was somewhat appeased. On Monday morning 16th July, the tapestry covered coffin was taken into Glinton Church for a brief service. All the village turned out as mourners. Mary had been so well loved by them all for long years, and many tears were shed that day. They carried her out and lowered into the grave next to her brother. 'Thank God,' thought Mrs Joyce. 'Now all William will see is a mound in this churchyard, when he returns home.' Ann, her eldest daughter was inconsolable. She could not face her brother for a long while.

James had been given a tall, stately headstone, and Mrs Joyce decided on as tall and fine a one for Mary, when the ground had settled, which took about a year from the original burial.

EIGHTEEN

John Clare was in the private asylum in Essex. Not one member of his family visited him there, and no one wrote to tell him of this tragedy. In 1841, on 20th July, three years after Mary's untimely death, he felt he had had enough, he walked out of the asylum without a word to anyone, and with only the clothes that he stood up in and a few books in his coat pocket, he found the main highway and walked almost all of the eighty miles home. His *The Journey out of Essex* is so familiar to so many that it need not be repeated here. His object was to be with his 'First Wife, Mary' and also to be with his 'second wife, Patty' and both their respective broods of children, of which he was father. When Patty met him on the road at Werrington, he did not know her and it was only with much difficulty that he was persuaded to enter the cart for the ride home. Passing through Glinton, he could see the church down the road. 'Where is my Mary?' he asked Patty. 'I want my Mary.'

He worried his wife and family so much that it was decided, behind his back, just to tell him that Mary was dead, but not ever to tell him the awful details of her death, for everyone in all the near villages knew the Joyce family, or had heard of them, and how the beautiful spinster daughter had died. They realised, quite rightly, that the shock would be too great for his system, and they feared a permanent madness. He would not believe his father, Parker, who had now come to live in the Northborough cottage, since his wife Ann had died just before Christmas 1835, still believing that Patty was only his second wife, and Mary still the first. So after a day or two, he wrote a prose account of his journey for Mary Clare of Glinton.

During that summer or early autumn of 1841, having satisfied himself of his cottage and land and flower garden and orchard, he began to take walks as the fancy took him. From his home, he could see the needle spire of Glinton church across the fields, and he recalled the old vestry school, and the lovely little girl he had first seen there, and an uncontrollable urge came over him to go to Glinton and find out if it were true what Patty had told him about Mary being dead. It was a lovely fine day, there were a few people in the main street where the church was situated, but he knew none, and none knew him. He gazed at the once familiar houses, and then he entered the churchyard by the gate facing the spire. There was a tall well-built man cleaning a spade, obviously the sexton. 'Good day Sir,' said the man.

'Good day,' responded John. There was a pause. Then John spoke, 'I would be so grateful if you could tell me, please, who now resides at the Joyce's Farm?'

'Why bless you Sir, 'tis the Joyce family, have been there for generations. And this churchyard be full of 'em! I buried some me self.'

'But who exactly lives at the farm?'

'There be the old lady, Mr James' widow, her son William whose farm it now is, and he is married and has a son called Adam.'

John Clare thought for a moment. 'Was there not an elder son, James?'

'That there was Sir, but I buried him meself, he lies at the edge of that path leading to the side gate, and his sister Mary, she be buried at his side, as was her wish, to keep him company!'

John Clare turned white and began to shake violently.

'Be you alright Sir? You can go into the church and rest ye, if you have a mind to.'

'Thank you, no, I wish to see the graves. Do they have headstones?'

'Aye, Sir that they do, tall fine carved ones they be,' and he pointed in that direction. The poet shook and stumbled his way down the path. He only saw the name James Joyce on the first stone, and read no further, but turned straight away to the newer second stone, with its boldly carved double scrolled top, and the large fine inscription, which read:

SACRED
TO THE MEMORY OF
MARY JOYCE
SHE DIED 14th JULY 1838
AGED 41 YEARS

He gave a smothered cry and fell to his knees on the soft turf. She had died the day after his own birthday! Good God, what irony there was in this vale of tears. The sexton had silently followed him, and now stood, rather embarrassed. 'May I help you up Sir?' he said at last, offering John his hand, who gratefully took it to help him to his feet.

'I did not believe she was gone.' A long pause. 'Can you tell me what happened?'

'Aye Sir, anyone in this village can do that for ye, burnt she was, her clothes caught fire late the night before, that would be Friday 13th. Could not save her, Sir, too badly burned.'

'Oh God,' moaned John, and put this hands over his face. The sexton saw the tears running through his fingers.

'Rest ye awhile, I pray you Sir,' he said, and taking the poet by the arm, led him to the church porch. 'Sit there if you will, or more private in the church.' With that the man left him.

He did now know how he managed to get home, in fact he could not remember walking home. All he knew was that Patty had told him the truth up to a point, but nothing else, though she must have known the full story. Entering his cottage, he dropped into a chair. Patty was preparing a meal. 'Where have you been this time, John, the children have been out looking for you.' It was some time before he could bring himself to speak.

'Glinton. I've been to Glinton. I've seen my Mary's grave.'

'Oh God,' breathed Patty. 'She was never your Mary, I am you wife, not her. You must forget her.'

'How can I forget? And why try and keep from me how she died?'

'Your father and I thought it was for the best, and I told the children the same. It's just a pity you can't be satisfied just being at home, and doing something useful, instead of chasing after these dreams. You can still make a go of this place. Other people would love to be in your shoes.'

'Well it's pity then they are not,' he retorted. 'I always knew who I loved, and why, and there's nothing can alter the fact. Maybe you should have wed that shoemaker your parents wanted you to instead of me, a worn out haymaker, as I was called on my journey out of Essex, ah, and a forgotten poet as well, that I am. Yes, Patty, I'm a complete failure, and none knows it better than I.' And he put his hands over his face and wept.

The remaining months at home only got worse. There were outbreaks of terrible anger and rage at his life in general, and finally Patty had to call in doctors.

John Clare was certified insane, due to years addicted to poetical prosing. At the end of December 1841, a small closed carriage drew up outside the cottage and several keepers from Northampton General Lunatic Asylum dragged him out of his home and bundled him into the carriage, which drove off at a smart pace. He would never set eyes on Patty or his home ever again. From that day until his death on the 20th May, 1864, John Clare the Northamptonshire Peasant Poet was kept in the asylum at Northampton. He was well looked after, but towards the end of his life he often said 'I want to go home' and also he had delusions of seeing dragons.

'Now Mr Clare,' they said to him, 'you know there are no such things.'

'That's what you think,' he thought. For dragons had flown to Glinton and caught his beloved first wife Mary, and by breathing fire at her, had thus set fire to her clothes and killed her. Only he knew that. No one else did. As there is little justice for any in this life, it is to be hoped that the souls of Mary Joyce and John Clare would be joined in union and love in the next world, and that their spirits will walk the woods and fields hand in hand forever in joy and harmony.

Epilogue

Patty's Tale

ONE

My name was Martha Turner; I was born at Tickencoat, at my parent's home, Walkherd Lodge, on 3rd March 1799.

My father was a cottage farmer, and our house was very isolated, but the countryside was so very pretty, I did not wish to live in a village, let alone a town. I never went to school. I could not read or write until after I was married. My husband John, he taught me. He was very clever in that line, in fact that was the only thing that he was good at, writing. Writing poetry that is, and, I blush to confess it – making babies! Of which I had more than my fair share! But that is what life and marriage is all about. It was he who made up the name that I am always known by – 'Patty'.

When we were courting, he said to me one day, 'I don't like your name, 'tis too severe sounding, not like you at all. And I have thought of a more suitable one for you.' 'Well what's that then?' said I. 'Patty' he replied. I was a bit taken aback, but I laughed and so did he, and we rolled about on the grass in the meadow, and then he had his way with me, and I became his Patty, and no more Martha, only to my family and friends.

Well, you see, I was only quite young then. He was quite a bit older, and had courted and had other girls before me, but I did not know that until much later. Like that girl that he met when only a schoolboy. Been in love with her ever since. I never seen her, but I know where she lived, and what her name was, Mary Joyce of Glinton! And that rather gives the game away, for my husband was none other than the poet, John Clare, and now I am known as the Widow Clare, and I was called that for long years before I actually became one.

But I must begin at the beginning. It was a Sunday afternoon, and I was returning home across the fields from visiting some friends, when I saw out the corner of my eye a small thin young man standing under a tree. I took no real notice of him, and continued quickly along the field path, but I suddenly felt I was being watched, so I half turned before I got quite out of sight, and I saw this same young fellow shinning up a tree! Well, I thought, he must be mad. What's he want to climb a tree for! If he falls and breaks his bones, there's no one to help him, is there? More fool him. Let him get on with it. So home I went and did not consider it further.

Some weeks passed, and I had almost forgot the incident, when one Saturday, early evening, I had been out visiting, and was nearly home, when I saw this same young man, and he was carrying a violin. So I slowed my pace to have a good look at him. He was short, and very thin, shabby of dress, a pale face with small deep set light blue eyes, and bright copper coloured hair. I could not help smiling at him, and he smiled back. 'Good evening,' says he. I smiled and nodded in return. 'I have seen you before, not far from here,' he said.

'Yes' I said, 'I do remember you. Are you a fiddler?'

'Well, I do my best. The gypsies they taught me to play my old Cremona.'

'I thought it was a fiddle,' said I.

'So it is, but 'tis called a Cremona, for that is the make of it, but 'tis still a violin.'

'Play me a tune, please,' I asked him. He smiled in answer, such a sweet smile, and then he began to play, and could he play! I had never heard anyone as good as he! I felt I wanted to dance and dance to the melody that he played.

After that I asked him his name, 'John Clare of Helpstone,' and I told him mine. 'Do you live far?' he asked. I said how far I judged it to be, and the name of our house. 'May I walk you there?'

'Yes' I said. So that's how it all started. He told me all about himself, the jobs he had done in the past, and he was now a lime burner at Casterton, but had high hopes of other things.

'What things?' I said.

'Ah, I'll tell 'ee next time, maybe', and he laughed. Of course, he meant publishing poetry, but I would never have guessed that one in a thousand years. So we said our farewells as he left me at the house door. I watched him go out of sight, and then I went in and told my parents of this young man who I had met. 'And he do play the fiddle lovely!' I told them.

'Fiddle?' said my mother, 'You just mind, my Martha that he don't "fiddle" with you!'

I knew what she meant and I laughed heartily at the jest, but she meant it in all seriousness, and then I was very young, and could not see the danger in this friendship, that soon became courtship, and fiddle me he surely did, and it was my undoing, but I see that I am running on a bit now.

Every Sunday he would walk over from Bridge Casterton to call on me, and sometimes, of an evening in the week as well. He said that the countryside around my home was the most beautiful that he had ever seen, far better than around his native Helpstone. I sometimes wondered what his home and Helpstone looked like. I never thought that I would end up living there for long years like I did do. Me and John loved to wander over the cow pasture and enter a large wood, where vast quantities of lily of the valley grew, wild, it was a favourite flower of mine. I used to love the scent and the purity of the tiny white flowers, and he would help me gather large quantities to take home and fill my flowerpots with them. He told me that he thought I was as pure as my flowers and that he really did love me, and we soon became secret lovers. My parents and also my friends were very cold towards John Clare. To them, he was only a lime burner, but had been other things, but had not a proper trade, like a certain shoemaker who had designs on me and tried hard to court me, but I did not fancy him and refused to encourage him in his desires.

The day came when, during our courtship, John told me of his hopes and dreams, of becoming a published poet. I was quite taken aback at this, I can tell you. I knew hardly anyone who could read or write, let along someone who could make up and write down proper poems and songs. John somehow had the feeling that this was his destiny and it was only a question of time when he would be in print and get the recognition that he craved. He read some of his poems to me and I did hardly credit that this young man had the ability to write such fine verses as these were.

The next thing was, he had taken steps to get a book published, and he had to go home to Helpstone to sort out his verses and see what these great men in London would do to help him. He did try and explain it all to me, all the people, their names, the real friends, the ones that only pretended to be friends, those that had only their own interest at heart – and not his. My poor head fairly swam with all these names, and in time I did come to meet with a few. When it became known to my parents that this young man was bringing out a book, they and my friends looked more kindly on our relationship, and now the shoemaker cut a sorry figure compared with John Clare, poet.

All was going along so well, until the day I found that I was with child, and then all hell was let loose. My parents called him every name under the sun for forcing himself on me, then their wrath turned on me for giving myself to him. They demanded he marry me. They did not want the shame of a bastard grandchild. There was a terrible scene when John did find the time to call on me again. And he had to promise to marry me. Then a date was set for his first book to come out, just a fortnight after his grandmother died, so I never met her. But she had been in the same way as I was then, with Parker who was none other than John's father! The old lady never did marry anyone and lived to be 82. That was going some, I can tell you. Not many people, poor people I should say, having a hard life, lived to that age. My parents said that as I had made my bed hard, so I must lie on it, but when John gave me presents of money to help with the situation, it did pacify them somewhat, although he did dither about the date of the wedding. He seemed sometimes reluctant to marry me, I knew not why, and there was little time to spare since I showed so much.

The next thing was. he had to travel to London to see and be seen by his publishers, and other people, patrons and writers. There was a grand lady named Mrs Emmerson, who did prove a real good friend to John, myself and our children. I did get to meet her, she came to the Helpstone cottage with her husband, very kind she was, but the way she spoke annoyed me somewhat, because she had such affected speech and put so much emphasis on every other word, as if to din it in to you, as if you did not understand the first time! I knew John's parents felt the same, but they dared not criticise so fine a person who bore gifts to us. And talking of gifts, why, if it hadn't been for her, I would not have had a proper wedding dress!

Yes, she sent me a gown from London, and it did conceal my expanding figure, for John was lackadaisical, and let the time run on so, and we was all so worried, but at last he returned from London, with such tales of the things he had seen and the people he had met, and, to top it all he had his portrait painted! His publisher, Mr Taylor, had paid fifteen guineas for it! I had never seen a sum of money like it. At last he married me, at Great Casterton Church. My Uncle John gave me away, my father did not feel well. I think the worry of my condition played on his mind, and mother stayed with him, but we was still a party of family and my friends, and after the ceremony, we walked just across the road to the inn for the wedding meal, that was paid for by Uncle John.

Then I went home to Walkherd lodge, to be with my family until the baby was born, and John returned to his parents at Helpstone, for there was much to do with his writing for a second book of poems, people calling, letters to be answered. I took off Mrs Emmerson's wedding gift and carefully put it away. In later years with all the daughters I have had, I did think to make other clothes from it, but I did not, and now, at the end of my life, I wish to be buried in it, when I am laid to rest with my children who are already gone, in Northborough churchyard, at the back of the high altar, in a long quiet, private line of graves. But I am running on many years in the future. We must go back to the early summer of 1820.

My husband would come over to see me whenever he could spare the time, and on 2nd June, I gave birth to our first child, a daughter, named Anna. John was overjoyed. It was quite some time before John came to fetch us to live with his parents and his sister Sophy in the old Helpstone tenement. He had so often called it a hut, and to be truthful, it was not much better. The walls were thick and strong to keep out the cold, and it was heavily thatched. The inglenook fireplace was its best feature. You could sit right inside and watch the food cooking.

As soon as the cart stopped outside, his parents came out to meet us. The old man, Parker, could hardly walk, he was so badly affected by rheumatism. His mother Ann was dark as a gypsy, but kind in her own way. Then there was Sophy, I really did take to her, she was about my own age, very small and slight, with looks and colouring like her brother. It was a joy to have someone of my own age that I liked to have for a sister-in-law, and we got on together right from the start.

Well, life is strange, there we all were, total strangers to each other, having to live together in a small space, and having to make the best of it. Also I found it so different living in a village, so many people, so close at hand. I was always used to our isolation, and for a long time I missed the old home and my family dreadfully. But then I had a little child to take care of and I was only starting to learn. Old Ann, she helped me a lot. She had lost two other children, both girls, the first was John's twin Bessey, and then later the second daughter before Sophy was born.

TWO

There was much to do. John was so fond – no not fond, more like passionate – about his bit of garden and all the flowers and plants that he cultivated there. He had friends at Milton Hall, near Peterborough, and some plants came from there.

Then he had the idea to teach me how to read and write, since I had no schooling, and books were a mystery to me, apart from any that had pictures in them. So after a great while I mastered this new art. Old Mrs Clare always thought that reading and writing were akin to the black arts, like witchcraft, and yet when John was just a little lad, he had learnt at the dame school in the village, before walking the two miles along the bridle path across the fields to Glinton. Glinton, yes, and that was the cause of all my trouble, since it was there in the church vestry school he met Miss Mary Joyce, a farmer's daughter, and he fell in love with this girl, and stayed in love with her, despite being wed to me, and giving me all the children he did. And then there were all the other affairs. Yes. I am sorry to say he was not at all faithful to me, but that was how it was – I forgave him for the most part – he could not help it. It was all part of his nature. It made me angry to see so many of his poems addressed to 'Mary', for this was her. He knew a lot of girls and young women of that one common name, but it all came back to just one, Mary Joyce. She was the be all and end all of his fancy and affection. 'Mary the Muse' I calls her. But she has been dead and gone these many years, now, and she never did wed. So maybe she fancied my John, after all, but that we shall never know. Well, all I can really tell you is my life has been bearing John's children, cooking, cleaning and washing. But then, that is the same for women in my position all over the world, all down the centuries, and will be till the sands of time run out.

Poetry made my husband, and poetry was also his downfall. When a fit of rhyming came on him, he just sat at the old table his father had made, with sheets of blank paper, and a good supply of home-made ink, and scrat away for hours, and sometimes days, not knowing or caring what was happening around him. The muse had him in her spell. Then after that he would collapse exhausted, as if he had done the labours of ten men in the fields that day, but he would crawl off to The Bluebell pub right next door, and a bit more would be put on the slate besides his name. Then the poems were posted off, thankfully he did not have to pay for the postage. He had, however, to walk as far as Milton Hall, and they went from there to London. And he might get his dinner from 'Mr Grill' the chef, or bring a bite to eat back for us to enjoy.

Many presents of books came his way, and quite a number of visitors, if he was in the fields or the pub Sophy or myself had to run to fetch him. It always put me out when these grand persons rolled up in their gleaming carriages, stopping in the lane, for all our neighbours to gawp at. Many were so rude and insulting too, asking if he had done his courting in a pigsty, or even asking for a walking stick as a memento of their visit. If all these high and mighty folks had given us a £1 for every time we had the inconvenience of their calling, we could have kept a far better table of victuals and paid the rent on time.

Then there were all these trips to London. The money that cost! Thankfully that was paid by Mr Taylor, the publisher. But for all the good those visits did, he just might as well have sent us the money to spend on the children, for I was always with child. Then his sister got married, and her husband's name was William Kettle! Yes, and poor Sophy, she was always in the family way, and whenever I said to my John, 'Sophy's going to have another,' he would look at me and say, 'That Bill Kettle's been on the boil again!' and laugh and laugh.

'You can talk!' I says to him, 'You be just as bad!' and he was too. Couldn't leave me alone, or any pretty face or trim figure he happened to spot, and seduce if he could. And there was one young woman, quite genteel she was, so he says, who was a governess at a grand house, and quite threw herself at him and wanted to run away from her employers, and the safe, comfortable job and house, and follow my John wherever he went. Well, the neck of some people! They don't know which side their bread is buttered and that's a fact.

Our marriage had many ups and downs. John had bad bouts of illnesses, as did our children, and we all feared for each other's lives. Money was always in short supply, despite his books being a great success, as they were in the early days, and he wrote and published several volumes. The one that gave him the most trouble was *The Shepherd's*

Calendar, but so many folk have said to me that it is his finest book. It took years to write, re-write and correct and alter before Mr Taylor and Mr Hessey published it.

I lived in Helpstone, in the cottage where my husband was born, from 1820 until the spring of 1832, just 12 years, and then we moved away to the village of Northborough to a newly built large cottage with two acres of land, leaving old Mr and Mrs Clare behind in their tenement. It was a big change for me. No near neighbours, and so much space, and all that land, well, I thought we were in paradise. But not my, John. Oh dear, no. He could not seem to settle. He made a good garden, he did make an effort to become a cottage farmer, but nothing seemed to go right for him. And across the fields, he could see the tall needle spire of Glinton church that reminded him of his boyhood and of Mary Joyce.

One day, some months after we moved it, I was washing in the kitchen, John was upstairs writing, in front of the one small window that faced the lane, when suddenly he gives a shout and nearly falls down the stairs, being in so much haste to get out of the door. I thought that he had seen a carriage with gentry coming to call, as they so often did, but no, this was something different, for instead of disappearing down the fields out of sight, he dashed round to the front of the cottage, and down the lane towards the centre of Northborough, as if the very devil had taken possession of him. This was too strange, too curious. I left my work and walked slowly, a few yards down the lane. He was almost out of sight, but stopped abruptly and stood looking round like a lost sheep. He did not seem to know where he was or what he was doing. I got nearer, then I shouted 'John, what ails you?'

He turned and saw me. 'I am coming, Patty', and we returned home together.

'I know I saw her,' he kept saying.

'Who?' I asked.

'Mary!!!' he cried out. 'My Mary, I saw her, I did, I know I did, she was no dream, she was real!'

Oh, my God, I thought, him and that bloody woman, why the hell don't he forget her. A pity she don't get married and go and live somewhere else! But if wishes were horses, beggars would ride. No such luck.

Well the time passed and he could not take to Northborough, why I don't know. There was no comparison between the old place and this. He wrote and he wrote, and then he got another book published in 1835.

Then just before that Christmas, his mother died, and he was plunged into black despair, and it was decided that his father should come to live with us, and give up the old Helpstone home, and so it was. Times were hard, short of money, short of food and John's state of mind deteriorated. The doctors were called in, the old friends, the publishers, and patrons were all concerned for his well being, and it was suggested he go into a private asylum in Essex, in Epping Forest. It was all settled, and paid, and my husband went. There was no money to go and visit, but there were letters.

The following year, in the summer, July it was, there was a terrible accident, a death by fire, and it was none other than that woman. Mary Joyce of Glinton. She was 41 years old. Doing a job near the fire, and her clothes caught light. That was a real shock I can tell you. And, of course, I never let my husband know. She had been dead and buried these three years past, when one of my neighbours and his wife stops at our cottage, and runs up the path to say they have seen John himself near the bridge at Peterborough, filthy, covered in dust, walking home, and looking ready to drop down dead on the road! So my son and I borrowed a horse and cart and sets off to meet him. We saw a small, stooping little man at Werrington. He looked so old and changed but I knew my John. I stopped the cart and ran and grabbed hold of him, 'John, John, 'tis me, Patty!'

'Who?' says he.

'Your wife, Patty!' says I.

'My wife's Mary Clare of Glinton!'

Oh my God I thought, he has gone mad. 'No John, you married me, and I'm Patty,' and I got hold of him and bundled him into the cart and off we went. When we got to Glinton, I had the biggest job in stopping him getting out of the cart.

'She's dead,' I told him.

'I saw her a twelve month since,' he said.

'No, you did not. Mary is dead and gone.'

We at last reached our cottage at Northborough, and finally he realised it was his home, and family, and his old father, too. I got him food and drink, and boiled water and helped him get washed, and put clean clothes on him, and he sat and rested with his feet in soak in a bowl of water. His shoes were in such a state, they were not repairable. He still could not take it in that Mary was dead, and we dared not tell him any details, it were too shocking.

Then a few days later he began to write an account of his journey and escape from the asylum, and it was addressed to Mary Clare, Glinton – of course, it was never sent. The weeks passed, and he got his strength back, he began to enjoy being at home again, what with all the family to care for him, and the pleasure he took from seeing his flower garden again, and the orchard and fields. Then, he began to wander off on little walks, gradually getting further and further.

Then one late summer day, I got real worried where he was. He had been gone so long, and then finally he did return, and the look on his face! I knew there was trouble! 'Where have you been John?' I asked. 'Glinton' he said. Oh God, oh God, he knows, he knows! Yes and he did know! He had seen her grave and found out how she died.

Well, after that we all had a sad time with him. He went downhill from then on. Fits of rage like you never saw. I could not stand it, and I called in the doctors. They decided he was insane and must be put away for his own sake as well as ours. It was organised to send him to Northampton General Lunatic Asylum, and just after Christmas 1841, there came a knock at the door, and there were several man from the asylum come to take him away. We all cried, he did not want to go, there was a struggle, but they dragged him down the path to the carriage, bundled him in and off it went. More than twenty four years went by before I saw my husband's face again, and then it was an old man's face, cold white and still, laying there, in that coffin in The Exeter Arms pub in Helpstone.

What a funeral that was! I think the whole of Helpstone and the other surrounding villages all turned out, and the church and graveyard were packed with people. He thought he had been forgotten, but at the end it proved that was not the case.

So now I really was, what people had been calling me for long years, 'Widow Clare', and I am getting old and tired. I have always tried to look after my family and my home, and also to be helpful and kind to my friends and neighbours. I have had great hardships. Quite a number of my children are dead, and I am full of sorrow that I have survived them, but I do feel a change coming on, and maybe 'twill not be a great deal longer before I too join them. It is now January 1871, and I am staying with my daughter, Eliza Louisa Sefton, at Spalding, and she named her daughter after me, Martha, and yet, strange to tell, folks calls her 'Patty', as my poor husband, John Clare, the Northamptonshire Peasant Poet called me. God rest his soul.